DEVIL'S GOLD

A BLACK ROSE MYSTERY, BOOK 1

AMANDA MCKINNEY

HH TISEVICH

Paperback ISBN
eBook ISBN 978-0-9995553-0-9

Amanda
MCKINNEY
AUTHOR OF SEXY MURDER MYSTERIES

https://www.amandamckinneyauthor.com

DEDICATION

For Mama, always, and forever and ever.

ALSO BY AMANDA MCKINNEY

Lethal Legacy

The Woods (A Berry Springs Novel)

The Lake (A Berry Springs Novel)

The Storm (A Berry Springs Novel)

The Fog (A Berry Springs Novel)

The Creek (A Berry Springs Novel)

The Shadow (A Berry Springs Novel)

The Cave (A Berry Springs Novel)

Devil's Gold (A Black Rose Mystery, Book 1)

Hatchet Hollow (A Black Rose Mystery, Book 2)

Tomb's Tale (A Black Rose Mystery Book 3)

Evil Eye (A Black Rose Mystery Book 4)

Sinister Secrets (A Black Rose Mystery Book 5)

BESTSELLING SERIES:

Cabin 1 (Steele Shadows Security)

Cabin 2 (Steele Shadows Security)

Cabin 3 (Steele Shadows Security)

Phoenix (Steele Shadows Rising)

Jagger (Steele Shadows Investigations)

Ryder (Steele Shadows Investigations)

★ *Her Mercenary (Steele Shadows Mercenaries), coming May 2022* ★

AWARDS AND RECOGNITION

JAGGER (STEELE SHADOWS INVESTIGATIONS)
*2021 Daphne du Maurier Award for Excellence in
Mystery/Suspense 2nd Place Winner*

THE STORM
*Winner of the 2018 Golden Leaf for Romantic Suspense
2018 Maggie Award for Excellence Finalist
2018 Silver Falchion Finalist
2018 Beverley Finalist
2018 Passionate Plume Honorable Mention Recipient*

THE FOG
*Winner of the 2019 Golden Quill for Romantic Suspense
Winner of the 2019 I Heart Indie Award for Romantic Suspense
2019 Maggie Award of Excellence Finalist
2019 Stiletto Award Finalist*

CABIN 1 (STEELE SHADOWS SECURITY)
*2020 National Readers Choice Award Finalist
2020 HOLT Medallion Finalist*

THE CAVE
2020 Book Buyers Best Finalist
2020 Carla Crown Jewel Finalist

DIRTY BLONDE
2017 2nd Place Winner for It's a Mystery Contest

RATTLESNAKE ROAD
Named one of POPSUGAR's 12 Best Romance Books to Have a Spring Fling With

~

"My mouth literally hung open when I finished this book. You do not want to miss this one." -5 STAR NetGalley Review

Praise for the Berry Springs Series:
"One of my favorite novels of 2018." -Confessions of an Avid Reader, **The Fog**

"**The Woods** is a sexy, small-town murder mystery that's guaranteed to resonate with fans of Nora Roberts and Karin Slaughter." -Best Thrillers

"Danger, mystery, and sizzling-hot romance right down to the last page." -Amazon Review, **The Creek**

"Amanda McKinney wrote a dark, ominous thrilling tale spiked with a dash of romance and mystery that captivated me from start to finish..." -The Coffeeholic Bookworm, **The Lake**

"**The Storm** is a beautifully written whodunnit, packed with suspense, danger, and hot romance. Kept me guessing who the murderer was. I couldn't put it down!" -Amazon Review

"I devoured **The Cave** in one sitting. Best one yet." -Amazon Review

"**The Shadow** is a suspense-filled, sexy as hell book." - Bookbub Review

LET'S CONNECT!

Text **AMANDABOOKS to 66866** to sign up
for Amanda's Newsletter and get the latest
on new releases, promos, and freebies! Or, sign up below.

Amanda
MCKINNEY
AUTHOR OF SEXY MURDER MYSTERIES

https://www.amandamckinneyauthor.com

DEVIL'S GOLD

Despite being chronically late, occasionally disheveled and a tad disorganized, Dixie Knight is one of the top private investigators in the country, and when a young woman goes missing in the small, Southern town of Devil's Den, Dixie takes the case. She expected it to be another ordinary missing person case—until it takes a brutal turn.

While visiting relatives on his two-week leave, Marine Liam Cash bumps into Dixie at the local bar, and his attraction to her is immediate. When he becomes suspicious that Dixie's current case is connected to two unsolved murders in his hometown, he steps in to help investigate, and keep Dixie safe, whether Dixie wants him to or not.

As the bodies start stacking up, Dixie turns the town upside down looking for the killer—could it be the rumored witch that lives in the mountains; the rich, neurotic doctor's wife; or the perky, blonde receptionist at the local medical clinic?

Time is running out, and Dixie knows she has to put the pieces of the puzzle together before another body turns cold in Devil's Den.

1

*T*HE SILVER GLOW of the moon lit her way as she slipped silently through the woods, her eyes locked on the silhouette a few yards in front of her. A gust of ice-cold wind whistled through the tall pine trees, breaking the eerie silence of midnight.

He stopped.

She stopped.

Dixie peered through the binoculars and watched the tall, bulky man step behind a tree, his gaze fixed on the rickety log cabin just ahead of him—the home of her client, Beverly Clemens, who was terrified that her crazy ex-boyfriend, Emmett, was stalking her.

And it appeared that Beverly was right.

She pulled the night vision camera from her bag—*click, click, click,* then switched angles—*click, click, click.*

"I've got you now," she muttered under her breath. Just a few more pictures—preferably with a full-face shot—and her client should have no problem getting a restraining order against her obsessed ex.

Dixie slid the camera into her pocket and glanced at the

house. A dim light shone through a back window, its orange beam spilling onto the ground, illuminating the fresh dusting of snow.

It was a cold, quiet night—the calm before the snow that was promised to be on its way.

She wiggled the stiffness from her toes, yanked up the collar of her trench coat, and kicked herself for not grabbing a hat on the way out of the house. Although, at the time, she hadn't realized that an evening of casual surveillance would turn into a bone-chilling hike through the mountains. In the middle of the damn night.

Dixie narrowed her eyes and watched him. Watched him, watching her client.

Emmett was a big guy—she guessed over six feet, two-twenty, at least. Not someone she'd want stalking her, that's for sure. So far, this case had been the typical ex who couldn't let go, but there was something about tonight; something about the way Emmett had tromped through the woods, with purpose, with a sense of urgency, that had Dixie on edge.

Her sixth sense—her gut instinct—was telling her to stick around and to keep her head on a swivel.

Dixie reached into her bag, grabbed her thermos, sipped, and wrinkled her nose—nothing like tepid coffee to take the fun out of a stakeout. After shoving the drink back into her bag, she felt around for anything to give her a boost of energy. *Bingo* —a half-eaten Snickers bar. Like an addict needing a fix, she ripped into it, savoring the tingle of sweetness on her tongue.

The blustery wind whipped through her long, dark hair. Dead leaves spun up from the ground. Dixie wrapped her coat tighter, crossed her arms over her chest and leaned against the tree to take the weight off of her aching feet.

Suddenly—*snick.*

Dixie tensed from head to toe, her senses shifting behind her. It was a good bet she wasn't the only thing stalking something else in the woods. Her hand slowly slid to the hilt of her gun—the gun her father had taught her to use decades ago, the gun that she always kept with her.

As she slowly turned, a bat zipped past her. Fear shot like lightning up her spine, and she released a muffled *yelp,* biting back a scream.

Damn you, little devil bird.

Dixie swallowed the knot in her throat and took a deep breath. Her eyes darted around the dense woods that surrounded her. Dark shadows from the full moon danced along the forest floor, creepily swaying back and forth, playing tricks on her—The Great Shadow Mountains were certainly living up to their name tonight.

To some people, the light of the moon washing over the trees might look enchanting, magical, safe. But Dixie knew better than that. She knew that the Great Shadow Mountains were home to thousands of creatures, including bears, mountain lions, snakes, coyotes, and more bats than Dixie cared to think about. The miles and miles of woods were speckled with deep valleys and caves, which provided shelter for the animals, and plenty of places to hide. According to the legends, the mountains were haunted—full of ghosts and evil spirits. But perhaps most notably, was the legend of Krestel, a witch who lived deep in the mountains, casting spells on anyone who was unfortunate enough to cross her path.

Like most small, Southern towns, Devil's Den had its fair share of folktales, but Dixie didn't believe in Krestel, or the stories that the old cowboys told after too many whiskey drinks at the local watering hole. No, Dixie wasn't scared of ghosts or witches—just bats.

She released the grip on her gun, turned back around, and focused again on Emmett, still standing motionless behind a tree.

What the hell was he planning to do? Just stand there and watch the house all night?

Dixie blew out a breath and glanced at her watch—just after midnight.

Minutes ticked by.

An owl hooted in the distance.

Suddenly Emmett reached into his pocket, and a flash caught her eye—a glint of moonlight sparkling off the tip of a blade.

Her heart skipped a beat, her back straightened like a rod. "Whoa buddy, what're you planning to do with that...", she whispered.

He began to move through the woods, toward the house.

Her senses piqued.

She took off after him, silently stepping through the brush. A thick cloud floated over the moon, hampering visibility.

Dixie picked up her pace, her eyes locked on her target.

As Emmett stepped into the yard, her gaze shifted to movement inside the house. A silhouette passed by the window, holding a large bag. A trash bag maybe?

"Oh, God, *no*, Beverly, don't go outside."

Her heart began to pound.

She quickly looked back to where Emmett was standing only a second earlier—*shit!*—he was gone.

Shit, shit, shit!

She pulled the gun from her belt, jogged through the

woods and into the yard. Frantic, she looked from left to right.

Where did you go, where did you go...

Suddenly, a spine-tingling scream vibrated through the air. Dixie spun on her heel and sprinted toward the back of the house.

Another scream—this one had the hair on the back of her neck standing up. As she rounded the corner, she saw Beverly kicking and screaming, being dragged by her hair through the back door.

"Let her go!"

Startled, Emmett dropped Beverly, took one look at the gun in Dixie's hand and bolted toward the woods.

Dixie leapt onto the back porch. "Are you okay?"

With eyes the size of golf balls, Beverly nodded, her brown, disheveled hair sticking out from her head. "Yes, yes, oh my *God*."

"Go inside, lock the doors, and call the police. And, *do not* answer the door for anyone. Do you understand?"

A frantic nod.

"Go!"

As Beverly scrambled inside, Dixie took off like a rocket across the yard. She gripped her gun and pushed into a sprint, leaping over a rotted log and into the woods. Up ahead, she spotted him. Adrenaline surged through her veins, the ice-cold air burning her lungs.

She was gaining on him.

She thought of Beverly, and how if she hadn't been there, it was very possible that Beverly would be tucked into body bag this evening, instead of her bed.

She gritted her teeth.

Son of a bitch.

Dixie pushed harder—she was only a few feet behind him now.

He stumbled on the uneven terrain, and she lunged forward, throwing herself onto him. As they tumbled to the ground, the gun flew from her hand.

Fists flying, legs kicking, she caught an elbow to the jaw, sending a fresh rush of adrenaline through her. She answered back with right hook, connecting with his cheek.

"*Ow!* Get off me, *bitch*!" He threw her off of him and as she hit the ground, her hand swept past a cold piece of steel —her trusty friend. She gripped, and as Emmett scrambled to get away, she jumped up, grabbed his sweatshirt, and shoved the barrel of the gun into his neck.

"Don't even think about it."

He froze. "Who the *fuck* are you?"

"Dixie Knight, PI."

2

*D*IXIE MUTTERED A curse as her beat-up red Chevy slid on a patch of ice—narrowly missing the ditch—as she turned onto the driveway.

She slammed the brakes, leaned over the steering wheel and peered at the wooden sign lying on its side. Apparently, someone else had slid off the road, right into their sign—and didn't have the damn decency to pick it up.

Dixie paused for a moment, then with a groan, shoved the truck into park and got out. The freezing-cold wind stung her skin as she yanked a hammer and box of nails from the bed of the truck.

She stomped across the driveway, kneeled down, and wiped the snow from the sign.

Black Rose Investigations

The sign was broken at the base, and it wasn't like she was going to be able to hammer it into the frozen ground anyway. So she picked it up, turned on her heel, and slipped on another patch of ice—sending her feet flying into the air. The breath *whooshed* out of her lungs as she slammed into the ground.

"Son of a *bitch*." Dixie blinked, squeezed her face in pain.

With a grunt, she rolled to her side, face-to-face with the metal hammer that had flown out of her hand. She raised her eyebrows—missed a bullet with that one.

She pushed herself up, plucked the hammer and nails from the snow and walked—carefully this time—to the mailbox, and nailed the sign into the base.

Extra irritated now, she sent a menacing glare down the road before jumping back into her truck. Dixie cranked the heater and began to make her way down the long, rock driveway.

It was a dark, bleak morning. The light of dawn took refuge from the icy temperatures by hiding behind the dense clouds that had been spitting snow since the evening before. She glanced up at the leafless trees that had grown like a tunnel above the driveway—like witch's fingers, connected at the tips. Ice clung to the bare branches, and the flakes of snow that found their way through the snarl of branches slowly flittered down onto her truck.

Through the haze, the dark house came into view at the end of the tunnel of trees, looking creepier than ever in the gloomy morning.

Their office was a two-story, old stone mansion with massive stone pillars and a large balcony that overlooked the grounds. Creeping fig vines clung to the stone walls, stretching up to the roof. Gargoyles—yes, *gargoyles*—glared down from the peaks. The house had been purchased and completely renovated by Dixie's parents, decades ago.

Although it wasn't the most professional looking office building, it was perfect for the kind of work they did. Death and darkness were the norm at Black Rose Investigations.

Dixie glanced at the cars out front and muttered another

curse—yep, as suspected, her vehicle was the only one missing.

She was late. *Again*.

She pulled around the house, parked by the back door and glanced at her watch—eight twenty-one.

"Dammit."

Dixie turned off the engine, grabbed her briefcase, folders, cell phone and purse, and pushed out of the truck.

Her assistant, Raven Cane, met her at the back door. Wearing a form-fitted grey sweater, tight black jeans and heels, Raven looked like she'd just stepped out of a high fashion magazine. Her long, straight, brown hair was pulled back into a slick bun, accentuating her high cheekbones and big, blue eyes, framed by impossibly long lashes.

"Morning, boss." Raven handed her a mug of steaming coffee.

"Morning, and thanks." Dixie kicked the door closed and took a sip, hoping that a little Baileys had made its way into the cup. Nope—luck was *not* on her side this morning. "Did you see the damn sign?"

"Yes, I already made a note to get it replaced."

"ASAP. And go with some sort of indestructible metal or something."

"You got it."

Dixie pretended that she didn't see Raven wipe up the ice and mud that she'd dragged in from outside.

Always prepared for everything, Raven's incessant need for organization and structure were two of Dixie's favorite things about her assistant. While Dixie was a constant tornado, Raven was the calm after the storm, a perfectionist, keeping everything together. Sure, her assistant was a little high-strung—okay, a lot high-strung—but she was a workhorse, a *patient* workhorse, and she was a perfect match for Dixie.

"The meeting has already started."

"Figured." Dixie walked through the massive kitchen with dark hardwood floors and grey stone walls.

"By the way, hell of a job on the Clemens case. Another case successfully closed, boss."

"And a million more to go."

"How long had the ex been stalking her?"

"For weeks, apparently. But she didn't call me until a few days ago."

"And not a minute too soon. Were you able to get any sleep last night?"

Dixie shook her head. After handcuffing her client's crazy ex-boyfriend, waiting for the police to arrive, and then giving her statement at the station, she was on less than three hours of sleep. But it was worth it—it always was.

Dixie rounded the corner into the dining room, which they'd turned into the main conference room.

Her older sister, Roxy—impeccably dressed as always—sat at the head of the table, with a stack of papers in her hand. Her hair was pulled tightly in a long ponytail that ran down the back of her designer suit.

"Thanks for showing up."

Dixie cocked a brow. "Sorry, I was picking up the sign that none of you jerks had the courtesy to do."

"No, none of us jerks had the time—we all make it a priority to be on time for our weekly Tuesday morning meeting... at the *exact* same time, every *single* week."

Without missing a beat, Dixie quipped, "Or was it the fact that you didn't want to get mud on your brand new, eight-hundred dollar boots, dear sister?"

A few snickers sounded from the back of the room.

Roxy raised her eyebrows, a twinkle in her eye. "They're Italian leather, something you wouldn't know much about." She grinned. "Drink your coffee, I'm assuming you haven't replaced the broken maker in your house. Now, back to business..."

Her older sister was right on both counts—Dixie didn't care for designer labels, and she also hadn't replaced the ancient coffee maker that had finally broken a week earlier. And yes, she was a total bitch in the mornings without her coffee. She took a deep sip and pulled off her beanie, slinging ice and snow all over the table.

Her younger sister, Scar—short for Scarlett—grinned and tossed her a napkin.

Dixie winked and mopped up the mess.

Seated around a long, wooden table were the motley crew that made up Black Rose Investigations. Across from Dixie were Scar and her assistant, Harley, and at the end of the table sat Fiona, Roxy's assistant, and Raven. And sitting beside Dixie was their office manager and super genius, Ace Zedler, who lived on the second level of the office, free of rent in return for keeping an eye on the place while they weren't there.

As Dixie scribbled notes, Roxy continued with the meeting, which was a touch-base to review the current cases of the week, and discuss travel plans, if any. It was a recurring meeting that their father had started decades ago.

Born and raised in the small town of Devil's Den, the three sisters grew up traveling the world with silver spoons in their mouths. Their father, Clive Knight, was a highly decorated CIA agent who came from a political family, rich in both legacy and wealth—*lots* of wealth. Their mother, Star Knight, was a small-screen actress, who met their father while researching one of her roles. After Clive and Star got married, they immediately started a family and relocated to the south, to get out of the limelight and lay down roots. Star walked away from her career so she could stay home with the girls, while Clive traveled constantly for work.

After a long, exhausting and *dangerous* career with the CIA, Clive retired and started a private investigation agency, Black Rose Investigations—a name picked out by his wife.

Black Rose specialized in civil investigations, but accepted all kinds of cases including surveillance, fraud, corporate investigation and infidelity, among other, more obscure areas.

Dixie, Roxy and Scar grew up running the halls of the agency, earning their allowances by doing small tasks for their father, and learning the ropes in the process. Clive made it his life's mission to raise three strong, independent women who could handle themselves in any situation. At a young age, the sisters were taught the skills needed to become a private investigator, advanced self-defense techniques, and how to handle a gun.

After high school, the sisters followed in their father's footsteps, each majoring in Criminal Justice and graduating college with honors.

The pieces of the Knight family puzzle seemed to be falling into place until the day that changed the sisters lives forever—the day their mother and father died in a tragic plane accident on the way back from vacation.

In one day, the three sisters inherited a massive, multi-home estate and thriving business. And after ten long years of working their asses off promoting and growing the company, Black Rose Investigations had become one of the most prestigious private investigation companies in the country.

By appearances, the sisters could be triplets—each

having long, ebony hair, flawless porcelain skin, and killer bodies that women envied and men drooled over. They inherited their enchanting beauty from their mother, and their take-no-prisoners attitude from their father.

By personalities, the three sisters couldn't be more different.

Roxy, the oldest, was the glue that held the sisters together. Always cool, calm and collected, she handled the lion's share of the *business* part of their business. Roxy was the type of woman to keep her emotions tucked away, only to be released in the privacy of her shower, and even then, it was only a single, glistening tear. She was one tough gal, no doubt about it, and a hell of an investigator. Roxy had her father's analytical mind. She was able to put random pieces of a puzzle together that no one else could. Roxy worked outside the lines, always, and sometimes outside of the law to get the job done.

Scar, the youngest, was the more reserved, free-spirit of the sisters, and mirrored their mother the most. If Scar didn't have her head in a book, she was working twenty-four hours on her cases—the definition of a workaholic. Scar had an uncanny way of pulling information from the tightest-lipped clients and suspects, using her soothing and trusting nature—or *aura,* as she would call it. The local PD often called her to interview witnesses when they were at their wit's end. Her only fault was that she had a tendency to take her work home with her, becoming too emotionally invested in each case.

And then there was Dixie, the middle child, the only frugal sister, who felt like she never quite fit in. Always running to catch up, it seemed, Dixie was the type of girl that was always late, always forgetting things, always losing things, and, according to her sisters, always had her head in the clouds. But Dixie was smart. *Super* smart. Dixie had inherited two things from her father—his eye for the smallest details and pieces of evidence that were always missed, and an infallible instinct at a crime scene. Dixie saw things that others simply missed, and those "small things" had helped solve countless cases. Each of the sisters were highly sought-after investigators, but Dixie had a reputation all her own—*Eagle Eye,* as she was known.

3

*D*IXIE DRAINED THE last of her coffee and flicked on the light as she stepped into her office.

She tossed her purse on the floor, maneuvered around a stack of boxes overflowing with files, and sank into her leather chair. Before she could take a breath, Ace poked his head in... and wrinkled his nose.

"Dude, what's that smell?"

Dixie's eyes rounded, and a second of panic shot through her... she'd remembered to shower, right?

Yes, she'd definitely showered, and even dabbed on a little perfume that Roxy had brought her back from Italy. So according to the description on the box, she should smell like white calla lilies and not something worthy of a wrinkled nose.

She frowned and looked around, her gaze landing on a small pizza box under her desk. "Oh. Dammit, I forgot to toss the pizza."

Ace leaned against the doorframe. "From *Friday*?"

She shrugged and picked up the box from the floor. "What's wrong with three-day old pizza?"

"The scent, Dixie. The scent is what's wrong with it." He shook his head. "Why can't we hire a maid?"

Dixie powered on her computer. "We are absolutely *not* paying someone to do what decent human beings are supposed to do themselves."

Ace rolled his eyes.

"Besides, someone's got to feed Krestel."

"Krestel only eats little children."

"Or, your little girlfriends, who seem to disappear immediately after the first date." She winked. "How'd it go Saturday night?"

Ace pushed off the doorframe and sank into the only chair that wasn't covered in papers and candy wrappers. "She was boring."

"Boring? Pea-sized, bleached-blonde *Pepper* from the drive-in was boring?"

"Not every woman can be as beautiful as you, dear Dixie."

She laughed. "No, I'm saying that maybe you should go for a different kind of woman next time. Someone with a college degree perhaps, and maybe a real pair of boobs every once in a while... you know, mix it up a bit."

He gazed lustfully at the ceiling, "But life's so much more fun with them... blondes I mean."

She grinned. "Of course."

"Anyway, I don't think she took too kindly to my digs."

Dixie flashed her best sarcastic shocked face. "*Whaaat?* You mean she didn't like being brought to this dark, scary mansion after you took her to Tubby's BBQ?"

"I took her to Mario's Pizzeria, thank you very much. But yeah, after I told her the house was rumored to be haunted, she was creeped out through the rest of the movie."

"First, quit telling people this place is haunted, and second, what movie did you pick?"

"Deadman's Cross."

Dixie shook her head. "Probably not the best choice... in movie or girl."

Ace leaned back and kicked up his feet. "You're probably right. Anyone who doesn't like this palace ain't for me."

A legendary ladies' man, it wasn't uncommon for Ace to bring girls to the house, and Dixie got the vibe that he made a game out of the haunted rumors—spook the girls, so that he could draw them into his big, muscular arms and fight off any ghouls lurking in the shadows. But the sisters didn't bat an eye at Ace's late-night, extracurricular activities. Ace was as smart as a whip, with a double major in Computer Science and Criminology, and was indispensable to the company. His title "officer manager" was more of a façade, as most of the work he did for the company wasn't exactly on the books. Ace spent most of his time hacking into systems, files, phone records, public records, etcetera, to assist with cases. With dark hair, eyes as blue as the ocean, and a thick, muscular body, Ace was as handsome as he was smart, and was paid damn well for the work that he did for them.

Ace's phone beeped and he stood up. "Anyway, just wanted to say good morning. And by the way, bleached-blonde Pepper has a cousin you should meet. A Marine passing through town, visiting relatives on his two-week leave."

Dixie was already busy clicking through emails, giving Ace only half of her attention. "*Ha.* A jarhead in town for two weeks. Sounds like marriage material."

"Hey if you don't start seriously dating someday, I'm going to have to marry you just out of pity."

She gave him the side-eye and glanced at the door. "That'll do, Ace."

He grinned and turned. "Always a pleasure, Eagle Eye."

Dixie grunted.

Raven walked in. "Hey... whoa, it kind of stinks in here."

Dixie rolled her eyes and blew out a breath. "Okay, *okay*, I'll throw out the pizza just as soon as I get through these damn emails."

Raven walked over and plucked the grease-stained box off the desk. "I've got Hank on line two for you. Sounds wired."

"Wired?"

"Yeah, especially for nine in the morning."

Dixie frowned—it wasn't like the small-town lawyer to sound wired, no matter what time it was.

"Thanks, and don't forget..."

"I've already ordered a new sign."

"What would I do without you?"

"Drown in an endless pit of pizza boxes and Snickers wrappers." Raven gave her a wink before walking out.

Dixie grabbed a notebook and pen, and picked up the phone.

"Dixie Knight here."

"Dixie, it's Hank."

"Howdy Hank, what's got you out of bed so early?"

"Always the smartass. I've got a client that could use your services."

She leaned back in her chair. "Yeah?"

"Yeah. Does the name Suzie Blevins ring a bell?"

Dixie wrinkled her nose and searched her memory. "Ah, yes, the neurotic wife of that rich guy, the doctor. Lives up on the mountain. Fire-red hair, fancy sports car, carries that stupid small dog around with her all the time. No job, although that's just an assumption."

"Damn you're good with the details."

"That's why I pay myself the big bucks. So what's her problem?"

"She thinks her husband, John, a doctor at Den Care Clinic, is cheating on her with a young, blonde, twenty-something—a pharmaceutical rep that goes to his office. She says he's cheated on her before and is finally done with him." He paused. "I've never seen a woman have such hatred toward a man. She can't stand him. Anyway, apparently there's an infidelity clause in their prenup and she wants him caught so she can get his money after she files for divorce."

"Sounds like a charming woman." Dixie shook her head and leaned forward. "But nope. No way Hank. Wrong gal, I don't deal with that bullshit. I can patch you through to Scar, she's taken a few infidelity cases lately. Hang on..."

"Wait, Dixie..."

"Yeah?"

"I came to you for a reason... our young, blonde, twenty-something pharma rep was just declared a missing person."

She cocked an eyebrow. "Missing? As of when?"

"As of this morning. Didn't make it home last night. Her cell phone's off, and there's no sign of her whatsoever. Suzie is practically drooling with this new information—if her husband had something to do with it, she'd get every penny of his money."

"Name?"

"Lizzie Meyers."

"Last seen?"

"Leaving Den Care Clinic yesterday afternoon."

"The husband's clinic?"

"Yep."

"Who reported her missing?"

"Her parents. Apparently, she and her mom, Beth, text throughout the day, every day. The last time Beth heard from Lizzie was four in the afternoon, yesterday. Her mom texted her again around eight, with no response. Tried again multiple times through the night, and finally, drove to her place at five this morning—Lizzie wasn't there and showed no signs of sleeping in the bed."

"Maybe she just skipped town for a while, taking a break from life or something."

"No, her mom feels positive something bad has happened. Abducted, or worse. Mother's instinct."

"Hmm. Did the wife say if John was home last night?"

"She said they had dinner together, and after that, she thinks he didn't go back out."

"*Thinks?*"

"Big house."

"Do the police know about the alleged affair?"

"That I don't know. It's hot gossip though, so it wouldn't surprise me. Anyway, just find a link between John Blevins and Lizzie Meyers, and my client would be more than happy, and would pay handsomely."

It wasn't about the money for Dixie—it never was—and the last thing she wanted was to get caught up in some bullshit infidelity case. But a missing person? Here in Devil's Den? That was right up her alley.

She glanced at the forty-one unanswered emails glaring at her from her computer screen, and at the angry, blinking light on the phone, alerting her of unreturned calls. She really didn't have time for another case.

"I'll take it."

"Fantastic. I'll email you the wife's—Suzie's—contact information, and I'd like you to get started right away."

"You always do. I'll send you through to Raven to discuss payment."

"You always do."

She smiled.

Click.

4

*D*IXIE CLICKED OFF with Hank, waited a moment, and picked the phone up again.

"Den Care Clinic, how may I help you?"

"Hi, I'd like to make an appointment with John Blevins, please. This morning if possible."

"Name?"

"Dixie Knight."

"Just a moment..." *Click, click, click.* "I'm sorry, Dr. Blevins is all booked up today, we can get you—"

"No, that's fine. Has he made it into the office this morning?"

"Yes, just a few minutes ago, actually."

"Was he in yesterday?"

"Um, yes ma'am."

"All day?"

"Um, I'm not sure... I'm sorry, is there something—"

"Thank you."

Click.

Dixie pressed the intercom button.

"Raven, come in my office. And grab Ace, too. Please."

Beep. "You got it, boss."

Under a minute later, Raven stepped through the door with Ace at her side. Ace took a seat as Raven carefully pulled the papers and folders from the other chair, stacked them neatly on the file cabinet, and then sat down.

"Okay guys, we've got a new case."

Raven raised her eyebrows. "A *new* case?"

"Yes..."

"On top of the zillion you're already working on?"

"Yes..."

Raven shrugged. "Alright, what we got?"

"Does the name Lizzie Meyers ring a bell?"

Ace's eyes lit up. "Yeah, that hot pharma rep, big boobs."

Raven shook her head in disgust.

Dixie rolled her eyes. "Aside from the size of her chest, what do you know about her?"

"That's about it. Drives a white sports car. I've seen her around from time to time but we've never spoken."

"I'm surprised, considering the size of her chest."

Ace grinned. "Just waiting for the right time to strike."

"Well that time might have already passed—big boobed Meyers is officially a missing person."

"No shit?"

"No shit."

Raven clicked her pen and opened her notebook.

Dixie continued, "Suzie Blevins, wife of John Blevins MD, believes he is having an affair with Lizzie. She's hired us to confirm that. I accepted the case because I want to find our missing blonde."

"Last seen?"

"Yesterday afternoon."

"Does Suzie think her husband had something to do with Lizzie's disappearance?"

"She's hoping—if we confirm the affair, and especially if he had something to do with the disappearance, she gets his money after she divorces his cheating ass. But according to Hank, her lawyer, she *believes* her husband was at home last night."

Ace leaned back and crossed his ankle over his knee. "First order of business is to determine Doctor Cheats-alot's whereabouts for last night."

"Exactly. I just hung up with the clinic. He's already in today and was there yesterday."

"So we know he and Lizzie didn't skip town together."

"Exactly."

Raven looked up from the notepad. "What about the wife? Any chance she's involved? Jealous, neurotic wife kills husband's mistress?"

Ace shook his head. "She'd be the dumbest criminal on the planet to hire a PI to look into Lizzie's disappearance if she had something to do with it."

Dixie shrugged. "Or the smartest—maybe she covered her tracks well and wants all eyes *off* of her, and on her husband."

Ace nodded. "Or hired someone to do the job."

"That too. But remember we don't know if Lizzie is dead, just that she's missing." Dixie stood and walked to the dry erase board on the wall. "Okay, so as of this second, with what minimal information we have, John Blevins is at the top of our suspect list." She plucked the top from a black marker and began scribbling on the board. "Ace, I need you to verify that John was at home last night, or that he wasn't—that's step one. Then, we need to narrow down the window of time Lizzie officially went MIA—check her credit cards, see when her last transaction was, check her cell phone."

Ace nodded.

"Raven, I need you to dig up absolutely everything you can on Lizzie Meyers, her family, boyfriends, anything. And then look into John and Suzie, too, but spend most time digging into Lizzie's life."

"You got it. I'm assuming the cops are already on this. Have you spoken with Zander?"

"I'll call him today." Dixie's phone rang. "Okay guys, that's it for now. Let me know what you find."

***

Dixie yanked up her hood as she pushed through the back door. The snow was coming down in blankets now, sure to snarl the mountain traffic on her way into town. The knot on her hip—from her fall earlier in the day—reminded her to tread lightly across the slick ground.

She winced as she slid into her truck, grazing her bruised hip across the seat.

It had been a crazy, busy day and now all she wanted was a couch and a glass of wine.

Damn, damn, *damn*, it was *cold*.

After clearing the snow with the windshield wipers, Dixie flicked on the headlights, made her way down the driveway, and onto the narrow, curvy mountain road.

Twilight sat on the horizon, its bright colors fading behind the snow-covered mountains in the distance. Devil's Den was no stranger to snow, or any weather for that matter. The small, Southern town experienced all four seasons— steaming summers, fresh springs, crisp falls, and ice-cold winters. And, with almost six inches of snow already, this winter promised to be no different.

She leaned forward and clicked on the radio.

"...snow is expected to continue for the next three days, accumulating close to three feet by the end of the storm. Power outages are to be expected, and please, stay off the roads."

Her gaze shifted to the ice sparkling on the steep ravine that hugged the side of the road—it would be a hell of a time to go missing... assuming Lizzie Meyers was still alive.

According to Raven's research, Lizzie was a twenty-three-year-old pharmaceutical sales rep with a business degree and a penchant for knitting, red wine and pedicures—the kind with fancy designs and jewels, apparently. According to Lizzie's social media accounts, she was gregarious, to say the least, spending almost every evening out—at dinner, at a bar, at a friend's house, or hosting book clubs and wine nights. And, she appeared to be single.

An only child, Lizzie was born into a hardworking, blue-collar family who attended church weekly and gave generously to local charities.

Nothing led Dixie to believe that Lizzie had any substance issues, mental, or physical issues, or anything that would make her hang out with an unsavory crowd. Lizzie appeared to be the run-of-the-mill bubbly, former sorority girl who lived life to the fullest.

John Blevins, MD, on the other hand, was a Devil's Den native and a workaholic, and had been married seventeen years to Suzie, with no kids. Dixie had reached out to the wife earlier in the day, only to receive her voicemail. But that was okay, she'd track her down later.

As Dixie pondered all the possible scenarios surrounding Lizzie's disappearance, something deep in her gut twisted—a woman's instinct... telling her that this was going to be no ordinary case.

Her phone rang.

"Dixie here."

"Dix, it's Ace. I tried to catch you before you left."

"What's up?"

"I've got some info on Lizzie."

"Give it to me."

"The last transaction on her credit card was Sunday night, the night before she went missing."

"Where?"

"At Banshee's Brew liquor store."

"How much?"

"Seven dollars and ninety-three cents."

"Maybe a bottle of wine, for herself."

"Right—doesn't appear that she was buying for a social outing. Also, Raven told me Lizzie posted a few pictures Sunday evening of a coaster she was knitting, so I don't think she went out. Aside from that, nothing seems out of the ordinary."

"Okay..."

"I also looked into her cell phone—her last call was placed at eight thirty-one Monday night, the night she went missing."

Dixie's eyebrows shot up. "Please tell me you have the number she called."

"I do, but it's a burner phone—no name attached to the number."

"*Dammit.*"

"The call bounced off a local tower, though. So whoever had the phone was close by."

"A burner phone usually belongs to someone who has something to hide. Someone that's up to no good."

"Agreed—like someone plotting an abduction, perhaps."

"Agreed. Assuming she called her abductor, then she

obviously knew him. Or, at least, had been in some sort of communication with him."

"Exactly."

"Okay... now I'm wondering if John Blevins recently purchased a burner phone..."

Ace groaned. "That's going to take a *hell* of a lot of digging."

"What? Not up to the challenge?"

"I'll let you know what I find."

"Thanks, Ace."

Click.

Deep in thought, Dixie tapped the phone on the steering wheel, then clicked it on again.

"Devil's Den PD, Lieutenant Stone here."

"Zander, it's Dixie."

There was a brief pause against muffled voices in the background.

"I'd like to think you're calling just to say hi, or perhaps to offer to bring me dinner for helping you with your last case, but something tells me that this call has to do with a young, missing blonde."

She grinned.

A Devil's Den native, former college football star, and one hell of a handsome cowboy, Police Lieutenant Zander Stone was Dixie's go-to for information. Why? Because Zander's father and Dixie's father had been best friends for as long as Dixie could remember. Zander was practically family and Dixie had no problem using that to her advantage, and neither did Zander, when he needed information from her, too.

A PI's relationship with local law enforcement was always a very sensitive, slippery slope, full of blurred lines, red tape... and secrets. Zander was invaluable to her and they both thrived in their quid pro quo relationship. Thankfully, due to budget constraints, the small town of Devil's Den didn't have a detective, so she didn't have to engage in that pissing match with every case that she accepted.

"Do you think my life revolves around crimes, Zander?"

"I have absolutely no doubt that it does, you sicko. You need to get a boyfriend, Dix."

She laughed. "Wow, if that isn't calling the kettle black, buddy. Your last relationship was when? A hundred years ago?"

"Just waiting for the right one."

"The *right one* is a phantom, a mythical creature that exists only to make men like you reject every single woman that comes across their paths, only to end up being a miserable old bastard who spends their time hovered over the engine of some sports car—that they spent their life savings on—with a bottle of lube in one hand, and a can of Bud in the other."

"That reminds me, my dad says hi."

She laughed. "Anyway, yes, you read right through me. What do you have on Miss Lizzie Meyers?"

"You on the case?"

"You could say that. Have you searched her place yet?"

"Just left. And, no, it's not open yet. Still roped off."

"What'd you find?"

"Hang on." More muffled voices. "Hunter wants to know when you're going to let him take you on a date."

Dixie rolled her eyes and blew out an annoyed, impatient breath. "Zander, tell me what you found at Lizzie's."

Zander pulled away from the receiver. "She said tonight, and she can't wait." He turned back to the phone. "You know I can't get into that with you, Dix."

"Just give me your read."

"Hang on." He pulled the phone away again, and muttered something. A minute of silence ticked by, and finally, in a low voice, he said, "Okay, Hunter just left. Not much to read; doesn't look suspicious so far. No break-in, nothing. Car's gone. I talked to her family and friends, no one has any idea where she went—she didn't tell anyone she was going out Monday night. Look, I gotta go, be careful on the roads, okay?"

"Did you find fingerprints in her house? DNA? Anything?"

"I gotta go."

"What about her car? Have you located it?"

"Dix, I gotta run."

"What else did the parents say?"

"They're in shock, gave us nothing to work with."

"I heard she lives close to ol' Black Magic Balik."

Pause. "Dix, listen to me. Do *not* go over there, I'm serious. I don't need you walking all over the crime scene. We plan to go back first thing in the morning."

"Hmm... that leads me to believe you guys found jack shit."

"Jack shit would've been something."

She raised her eyebrows. Yep, they found nothing.

"You going to the Black Crow later?"

Shit. She'd forgotten that she promised to meet Raven and Scar for a drink. "Yeah, I think so."

"I might see you there and *do not* go over to Lizzie's, you understand?"

Pause. "Talk soon, Zand."

Click.

Dixie tossed the phone on the passenger seat.

No signs of a break-in, no car out front. Based on that information, and Ace's research, Dixie felt strongly that

Lizzie knew her abductor—assuming that's what happened —and willingly drove somewhere to meet him, or her.

Regardless, they were almost at the twenty-four-hour mark, and according to most missing person statistics, that did not bode well for Lizzie Meyers.

Dixie reached over, plucked a wrinkled piece of paper off the seat and read the address scribbled across it—903 Shady Oaks Lane.

She leaned forward and squinted to see through the snow. As the street came into view, she flicked on her turn signal and parked next to a sign that read *Shady Oaks Cottages*.

Shady was right. Dixie turned off the headlights and looked around.

Four, small, decrepit stone cottages sat in a row, surrounded by leafless, ice-coated trees that backed up to dense woods. A fresh blanket of snow covered the grounds, which were untraveled on as far as she could tell.

According to her research, only two of the four cottages were occupied. One home belonged to Lizzie Meyers, and one to a Devil's Den legend—Black Magic Balik. Dixie wasn't the type of girl to give rumors much thought—especially in her line of work—and witch or not, Marden Balik was the only potential witness on the evening that Lizzie Meyers went missing.

One potential witness—and one was better than nothing.

She grabbed her bag, her gun, yanked up her hood and pushed out of the truck. The soft scent of snow tickled her nose as she lightly closed the door.

Black smoke rolled out of the chimney of Balik's cottage. A dim light flickered between the tiny cracks in the boards that blocked the windows. Dixie cocked her head—why were her windows boarded shut? Hiding something, perhaps? Various symbols, including a moon and stars, and strings of crystals hung from the cracked awnings. Two black cats lay curled at the front door, their beady, orange eyes flickering through the darkness. A black crow perched in the tall tree beside the cottage.

Dixie shivered—the only thing missing was a bubbling cauldron out front.

Her boots sank in the snow as she made her way to nine-zero-three—otherwise known as Lizzie's cottage.

Yellow *Do Not Cross* police tape flapped against the old, wooden door. A brown welcome mat lay haphazardly to the side. Shrubs lined the front of the house, with just enough room for someone to hide behind and peep in the windows.

Dixie pulled out her flashlight and surveyed the area. Muddy boot tracks were everywhere—presumably from the police—no scratches on the door or the window latches, and no fresh fingerprints on the glass. She stepped away from the door and shined the light along the rock walls, a shimmering layer of ice reflecting in the beam.

Careful to avoid adding unnecessary footprints, she stepped along the shrubs and rounded the corner to the back of the house.

Each cottage had a small back porch that stretched to the woods. Basically, the cottages were a detective's nightmare, and a stalker's dream. Too many places to hide, too many access points. Too dark.

A small table and two pink chairs sat on the porch, next to a narrow door which Dixie assumed led to the kitchen. The shades were drawn in both windows.

Nothing suspicious.

Dixie walked around to the front of the house and after taking a quick glance over her shoulder, pulled a small silver tool from her bag—courtesy of her dad—and popped open the front door.

The scent of cheap potpourri slapped her in the face as she slipped on a pair of booties and latex gloves before stepping over the threshold.

The cottage was ice-cold, still, and lifeless.

After taking another glance behind her, she shut the door and flicked the lights.

The one-bedroom cottage was tiny, with a living room, a small kitchen, laundry room, and in the corner was a door that led to the bedroom and bathroom. Despite the rock walls and old hardwood floors, the cottage screamed bachelorette pad with a stylish white leather couch under hot pink pillows, a flat screen television, and multiple brightly colored paintings on the walls. It was clean, too, and tidy, and in Dixie's experience, people who were clean and tidy were less likely to make irrational decisions.

Dixie walked across the kitchen and glanced in the fridge—Chinese take-out, an open bottle of wine, chocolate bars—normal single gal grub. She opened the freezer and wrinkled her nose at the nauseating amount of Lean Cuisines. *Gross.* She'd rather eat cardboard than that shit, which, by the way, tasted just like cardboard.

The trash can was empty, with a fresh liner that smelled of lavender.

Lizzie's bedroom was more of the same—pink, pink, pink.

Vomit, vomit, vomit.

Dixie paused, narrowed her eyes. Strewn across the pink bedspread were piles of clothes—silk shirts, lace tank-tops and designer jeans. She glanced in the bathroom—makeup and beauty products covered the counter. A curling iron and hairspray lay in the sink.

Her eyebrows tipped up.

Lizzie Meyers had spent the last moments in her home primping and prepping for something—for something special.

To see a man, perhaps?

Could that man be John Blevins?

5

*D*IXIE PULLED THE door closed behind her and ripped off her gloves and booties. Snow whipped through the air as she stepped away from the cottage.

It was a quiet night—an eerily quiet night, with only the soft sound of snow falling onto the trees.

Her phone beeped in her bag, startling her—one new message from Raven.

At the Black Crow, you still coming?

Dixie looked at the time—almost eight. *Shit.* She was late. Again.

Contemplating, she scanned the cottages. Maybe just one lap around the cottages before she left.

After tucking her phone into her bag, Dixie flicked on her flashlight, looped her bag over her shoulder, and began walking toward the tree line, sweeping the light along the snow-covered ground.

No boot prints, no tracks. The heavy snowfall took care of that.

She passed Balik's cabin, and shone the light onto the surrounding trees.

The hair on the back of her neck prickled.

She paused, her hand instinctively sliding to the hilt of her gun as she slowly turned.

A silhouette emerged from the shadows. In a low, raspy voice, it said, "Damn cold to be outside."

"And damn ballsy to creep up on a woman with a gun."

"It ain't creepin' when you're on your own back porch."

"You must be Ms. Balik."

"I am."

Dixie released her gun and took a few steps toward the woman. "I apologize, you spooked me."

"Not the first. Who're you?"

"I'm a friend of Lizzie's."

Silence.

"It appears she isn't at home, do you know where she is?"

A moment passed before Balik reached up and turned on an outside light, casting a dim, orange-tinted glow across the back porch. No chairs, no tables, just a few candles and stones. Snowflakes drifted through the light and onto Balik's long, black robe and scuffed leather boots, as she stood rigid, at the edge of the porch. Her stringy, grey hair braided down her hunched back. She wore black onyx earrings that accentuated the large moles on her face and her small, beady eyes that made Dixie want to take a few steps back.

Black Magic? A witch? Now having met Marden Balik, the rumors weren't so difficult to imagine.

The woman coughed a hideous sounding cough. She took a slow, unsteady step toward Dixie and stared at her for a moment before saying, "Lizzie ain't around anymore."

"What do you mean *anymore*?"

"You know exactly what I mean, Miss Knight."

Dixie raised her eyebrows. "Have we met?"

"Here and there."

No, she definitely would've remembered that face... those eyes. How the hell did Balik know who she was? And if she knew her name, Dixie had no doubt that the woman also knew that Dixie was a private investigator, and not a concerned sorority friend of Lizzie's.

"Ms. Balik, did you see Lizzie last night?"

"I see a lot of things, you know what I mean."

Impatience simmered. "I'm afraid I don't. But one thing I do know is that you need a license to carry that revolver you've got tucked in the pocket of your robe." Dixie slid her phone from her bag and dialed the police station. "So unless you want to..."

A crooked grin cracked across Balik's face. "You've got fight in you, Knight. I like that." She paused and shrugged. "I might've seen a black truck driving by over the last few days."

"What kind of truck?" She disconnected the call and shoved the phone into her pocket.

"Nice one. New."

"Make? Model?"

Balik shrugged.

"When was the first time you saw it?"

"A few weeks ago. Drives by every now and again but never stops. Sometimes pulls in and backs out."

"What time of day do you see it?"

"Night, mostly."

Dixie's gaze cut to the woods.

Balik continued, "Miss Meyers was a troubled girl."

"How do you know that?"

"I know the sort. Weak, ignorant, self-conscious."

"You don't sound like a fan."

"I wasn't a fan of the many boys she'd bring around here either, and I made no secret about that."

"Sounds like a typical single girl to me. Did she have a boy over last night?"

"Not that I'm aware of."

"No one came to visit?"

"Don't think so."

"Did you see her, at all?"

Balik hesitated. "I saw her leave."

"Was she alone?"

"Yes."

"Did you two speak?"

"No."

"Where were you?"

"Inside."

"What time was this?"

"After sundown."

"I need a time."

"After dinner."

They stared at each other for a minute.

Balik continued, "I've got to go back in now. Cats need feeding." She turned, and Dixie noticed something fall out of her pocket. Something pink—*hot pink*.

"Ms. Balik?"

"Yes?" She stopped, but kept her back turned.

Dixie quickly swooped down and picked up the object. "It's interesting that you saw Lizzie leave, considering your front windows are boarded up."

Balik's shoulders tensed and a moment of silence slid by. Finally, she turned her head, the steep bump in her nose highlighted by the dim background light. In a low, menacing voice, she said, "You're going to need that fight you've got in you, Miss Knight. Every bit of it." And with that, she stepped into her cottage and shut the door behind her.

Dixie slipped behind the wheel of her truck and clicked on her cell phone.

"Ace here."

"Ace, it's Dixie." She started the engine and cranked the heater.

"Dixie dear, to what do I owe the pleasure?"

"What do you know about Marden Balik?"

"*Marden Balik?* You mean ol' Black Magic Balik?"

"Yep."

"I know enough to stay the hell away from her. I heard she's part of Krestel's coven deep in the mountains—heard she does voodoo and shit."

"I don't care about the rumors *and shit.* What are the *facts* about her?"

"Rumors aren't necessarily untrue, you know, Dix. Anyway, Balik's a widow. Her husband died forty years ago after contracting a rare disease, and passing away within twelve hours."

"A *rare* disease?"

"Yep, and it was right after he'd told Marden that he was leaving her, for her *twin sister,* Agnes. He'd been cheating on her with her own sister."

"Bullshit."

"No shit... and..." Dixie heard him do a drumroll with his fingers. "For the cherry on top—Agnes, her sister, went missing a week later, never to be seen, or heard of again... *or so the story goes.*"

Dixie shoved the truck into reverse. "You're joking."

"Nope."

"So Balik's sister, Agnes, who was Balik's husband's mistress, is a missing person?"

"Yep."

"Pretty damn interesting."

"Yeah, it's a forty-year-old cold case, and a pretty creepy story if you ask me."

"Well, I ran into Balik tonight while checking out Lizzie Meyer's apartment."

"Maybe the witch has got Lizzie locked down in her basement... or in a simmering pot of stew with rabbits and puppies. Cute ones. Cute little puppies."

"You're sick."

"Thanks. Did you find anything?"

"A pink hair tie that fell out of Balik's robe."

"Uh, not exactly a smoking gun. You're thinking it's Lizzie's?"

She paused. Did she think it was Lizzie's? "Ms. Balik isn't exactly a pink kind of gal. Doesn't fit."

"You shouldn't be poking around that witch's house. I'm serious, Dix."

"Give me a break."

"Alright but don't say I didn't warn you."

"We need to find out if John Blevins drives a black truck. Balik said she's seen one driving by."

"A black truck? What's the make, model?"

"A newer model, that's all I know."

"No problem, will do. You going to the Black Crow?"

"On my way now."

"See ya there."

Click.

As Dixie pulled onto the road, a chill skirted up her spine and she glanced in the rearview mirror.

Through the pitch-black night, she saw Balik's silhouette standing in front of the dark woods. A small flame illuminated her wrinkled face, and beady, dark eyes as she lit a cigarette and watched Dixie drive away.

6

*D*IXIE WIPED THE fog from her windshield as she pulled into the gravel parking lot. The heavy snow had turned into an official snowstorm, with just enough visibility to make the drive home interesting.

She glanced at the clock—eight-thirty.

An hour late.

Dammit.

The parking lot was surprisingly crowded for a wintry Tuesday night. Dixie pulled into a spot between two jacked-up duallys with American Flags mounted to the beds, and slid on a patch of ice, barely tapping the Black Crow Tavern sign with her bumper.

"*Shit.*"

It was a bad day to be a sign.

She backed up a few inches, got out, and peered at the old, wooden sign—no marks.

Phew.

The low moan of a Willie Nelson song danced through the air as she pushed through the front door and inhaled the sweet scent of cedar, beer, and leather.

The Black Crow Tavern was a small, country bar located on the peak of Shadow Mountain. Once a log cabin hunting lodge, the bar had been purchased and renovated by none other than Zander Stone's grandfather, Chuck, a Devil's Den police veteran. The bar was frequented mainly by locals, and was a regular cop hangout, thanks to the owner. It was the type of bar where everyone knew everyone, *and* their business.

Old road signs and flickering lanterns hung from the log walls. Brown leather booths lined the walls, and custom-made wood tables and chairs speckled the main floor. In the back were a few pool tables, dart boards, and a small stage ready to showcase local bands, or brave drunks on karaoke night. Behind the wooden bar was a stone wall, holding hundreds of liquor bottles. But without question, Dixie's favorite amenity was the massive stone fireplace.

"Hey Dixie, nice of you to slide in."

She winced and turned toward the bar. "Sorry Chuck, if there's any marks, I'll pay for it."

The police veteran chuckled, accentuating the deep laugh lines around his bright blue eyes. "Do you know how many times that sign's been hit? If I got money every time someone slid into it, I wouldn't be working here. Jack and Coke?"

"Make it a double."

"You got it, dear." He nodded toward the back of the room. "Your girls are in the back. I'll bring your drink to the table."

"Thanks, Chuck."

Dixie maneuvered through the tables, nodding at people she knew, and careful to avoid those she didn't care to make small talk with.

"Hey, Dix!"

Seated in the corner next to the fireplace, were Raven and Harley, and a half-drunk pitcher of beer centered around a few empty shot glasses. No one could argue that the ladies of Black Rose knew how to handle their liquor. Men, on the other hand, was a completely different story.

"What are we celebrating ladies?"

"Tuesday."

"I'm in."

Chuck walked up and slid her drink across the table. "Here you go, Dixie girl."

Dixie smiled. "Thanks, Chuck."

With a wink, he walked away.

"Slick as shit out there, huh?" Raven sipped her beer, which was neatly wrapped in a napkin to keep the condensation off her hands, of course.

Harley shook her head, her curly, chestnut brown hair bouncing on her shoulders. "Only gonna get worse. Stan the weatherman said we're in for a few more feet before the week's over."

The newest member of the Black Rose team, Harley was born and raised in Devil's Den, and was a no-bullshit, tough-talking Southern gal. Prior to joining Black Rose, Harley was the go-to forensics photographer at Graves Laboratory—a local, private, full-service forensics laboratory—and was hired by local and federal agencies to photograph crime scenes in the tristate area. Harley was known for her quick wit and keen attention to detail at a crime scene. Dixie's younger sister, Scar, hired Harley as her assistant after working with her on a case involving a local kidnapper.

Dixie took a deep sip of her drink, savoring the tingle of the liquor as it slid down her throat. "How's the case going?"

Harley rolled her eyes. "You mean Crowley's innocent, little house fire?"

"Yeah, that one."

"Innocent my ass." Harley took a gulp of beer. "That old bastard had just spent the last penny of his wife's inheritance at the casino. He blew up the damn house for the insurance money... now we've just got to prove it."

"And killing his brother-in-law in the process."

"Yep."

"Did you speak with Chief Cage? Any signs of arson?"

"I've got a call scheduled with him first thing in the morning. Scar and I are going to do surveillance in an hour."

"Be careful, Crowley's got a gun arsenal the size of Texas."

Harley cocked an eyebrow and grinned. "So do I."

Dixie laughed and turned to the sound of chairs scooting across the hardwood floor behind her.

"Howdy ladies."

Ace pulled two chairs up to the table, one for him, and one for Roxy who was jabbing away on her cell phone, as usual.

"Hey, Ace. Who's she talking to?"

"Potential client. New York."

"Five bucks she takes it." Roxy was known to take jobs that were in close proximity to luxury clothing stores.

"Make it twenty."

"Have you found John Blevins's receipt for a burner phone yet? Or, figure out if he drives a black truck?"

"Can't a guy have a quick drink? I'm working on it, sheesh."

Roxy clicked off her phone and slid into the chair.

"Dammit it's cold out there." She plucked off her red designer gloves and gave her drink order to Chuck.

Ace slid into the chair next to Raven and pulled off his baseball cap. Always the flirt, he turned to her with a wink. "Hey, sweetheart."

Raven slid him the side-eye. "You're flinging snow all over the table."

He leaned in. "Oh, come on, live dangerously once in a while, Rave."

"And by live dangerously do you mean dating every warm-blooded female in town and then breaking their hearts? I'm telling you Ace, one day you're gonna break the wrong heart."

Dixie leaned forward. "She's right, Ace... there still might be time to salvage your last date with... what the hell was her name?"

Ace squinted as he looked toward the front of the bar. He closed his eyes and shook his head. "Pepper. Her name was Pepper, and speak of the freakin' devil."

Dixie glanced over her shoulder as the front door opened.

A gust of wind swirled snow around his massive body as he stepped over the threshold.

Her heart sank to her feet. Her attraction to him was immediate. Visceral. Every sensor in her body reacted to him.

Looking uninterested, at best, he casually scanned the room.

His eyes locked on hers.

For a moment, they stared at each other, somehow forming an immediate connection through the loud, crowded bar.

Before Dixie could catch her breath, a young blonde—presumably Pepper—grabbed his hand and dragged him to the bar.

"Holy *shiiiiiiiiit*."

Dixie turned as Raven jokingly wiped the drool from Harley's mouth.

Roxy shook her head. "That is one sexy, *sexy*, man."

Ace rolled his eyes. "Get a grip ladies. This isn't about you and your raging hormones right now, this is about me, and the fact that the chick I blew off, just a few hours ago, just walked through the front door."

Dixie picked up her ice-cold drink in an attempt to cool the heat running through her body. "Who's the guy?"

"Her cousin, Liam. The Marine I told you about earlier, from Louisiana. He's here on his two-week leave."

Harley frowned in disappointment.

Roxy snapped her fingers. "*Dammit*. Only two weeks. Thought we had a new man in town."

Dixie glanced back toward the bar.

A Marine... yes, he definitely looked like a soldier. A warrior. His chestnut brown hair was cut short, emphasizing his strong features and thick neck. He wore a thin, grey T-shirt under a worn leather jacket—which, if she had to guess, concealed a firearm of some sort—faded jeans, and scuffed combat boots.

She watched Chuck slide him a beer and, as if sensing her, he glanced over his shoulder.

And, again, they locked eyes before Pepper pulled him away, again.

Dixie turned back toward the table where the sexy man in town was no longer the hot topic. Instead, the conversation had switched to crime, murder, and chaos, as it always seemed to with this group.

Feeling out-of-sorts, Dixie drained her drink and pushed out of her chair. "I'm going to get another drink."

She turned and walked face first into a thin, grey T-shirt and rock-hard chest.

7

"*OH. OH, I'M* sorry." Dixie looked up, into the whiskey brown eyes that had hypnotized her from across the room just seconds before.

He smiled, his eyes twinkling.

Pepper stepped forward. "Hey, you're Dixie Knight, right?"

Dazed, Dixie took a step back, peeled her eyes away from the Marine's smoldering gaze, and turned toward Pepper. "Yes. I'm sorry, I don't think we've—

"Pepper." They shook hands. "Nice to meet you. I've heard so much about Black Rose and all the crazy stories. It must be so cool to be a private investigator."

Fighting an eyeroll, she smiled. "It can be."

"I was just at your office Saturday night... uh, I'm a... friend of Ace's."

Dixie glanced at Ace, who was shrinking in his seat. "I won't hold that against you."

Pepper laughed. "Thanks. Oh! I'm sorry, this is my cousin, Liam."

Her eyes met his as she slid her fingers over his large,

calloused hand—and was met with a firm, commanding handshake.

"Nice to meet your chest."

He grinned, and with a hint of a Southern drawl, said, "I'd think a private investigator would be more aware of her surroundings."

"And I'd think a Marine would do a better job of maneuvering out of the way."

His grin widened. He took a swig of beer, watching her over the rim. "Going to the bar?"

"Yep."

"I'll join you."

Dixie could feel the stares from the group as she walked away from the table, side-by-side with the sexy stranger. She was definitely going to catch shit from the girls later.

They stepped up to the bar and Dixie set down her empty glass as Liam casually leaned against the bar. He looked down at her with a penetrating gaze, a confidence, a swagger that made her feel like the only woman in the room. Her pulse picked up, and tiny warning bells sounded in her head telling her to be careful—this guy had charisma, and she had no doubt she wasn't the only woman to notice.

"So... a private investigator?"

"Black Rose Investigations, at your service."

"I didn't think most PI's carried guns." He glanced down at the barely visible bulge in her coat.

Her brow tipped up. "Nice eye."

"It's the job."

Chuck walked up, wiping his hands on his apron. "Another Jack and Coke, Dix?"

"Yes, sir."

"Another beer for you?"

"I'm good for now, thanks." Liam said, his eyes never leaving her.

Chuck nodded and walked away.

"I've heard stories about your dad, Clive Knight."

"You have?"

"Yeah, hell of an agent. Legendary."

"Thanks, and yeah, he was."

"You ever think about joining the CIA?"

"No."

He cocked his head. "No?"

"No. I caught the PI bug pretty young." Her gaze shifted to a pair of rowdy cowboys in the corner. "There was never a question of what I wanted to be." She looked up at Liam. "How about you? Always wanted to be a Marine?"

"Yes, ma'am. Like you, there was never a question."

Dixie turned fully to him, and titled her head. "You're from a military family, aren't you?"

"What makes you say that?"

"Aside from the fact you just called me ma'am, it says a lot about you that you're using your leave to visit relatives, instead of getting drunk on some beach somewhere. Most military families are extremely close-knit and loyal." She glanced at his arm. "I also caught a glimpse of that tattoo you've got on your forearm—family crest?"

With a gleam in his eye, he nodded, obviously enjoying her assessment of him.

"And, I'd guess you've followed in your father's footsteps, who was also a Marine."

"You're correct on all counts, Miss Knight—it's in my blood. And you're pretty damn observant."

"It's the job."

He grinned, sipped his beer. "What's a day in the life of a PI?"

"What isn't? Honestly, a little of everything."

"But Black Rose is no run-of-the-mill investigation agency. You're more than background checks, and finding Mrs. Bertha's lost cat."

"That's right... how do you know so much about us?"

"You're not the only one who pays attention."

Dixie stared at him for a moment. Her eyes pulled like magnets to his lush lips, and her heart skipped a beat. She turned away and picked up her drink—which was empty, *dammit.* She twisted the cold glass around in her hands.

"Yes, we're more than finding Mrs. Bertha's lost cat. We specialize in criminal activity, mostly. But we'll take random cases here and there. Cat's and all."

"Missing persons?"

"Yes, missing persons."

"Find Lizzie Meyers yet?"

She paused, narrowing her eyes at him. "For someone just passing through town, you sure seem to know a lot about Devil's Den."

The corner of his lip twitched, a thinly veiled smugness across his impossibly beautiful face.

Chuck delivered her drink, and took the empty glass from her hands.

"Thanks, Chuck." She sipped, feeling Liam's eyes on her. "Anyway, I'm sure the local PD will locate her soon enough."

"Okay, keep your secrets Miss Knight, but you're past the twenty-four-hour mark. Seems to me you could use all the help you could get."

"Hey, Dixie girl." Zander walked up and slung his arm around her shoulders—a not-so-subtle protective gesture aimed toward the stranger standing next to her. "Who's this?"

"This is—

. . .

"Liam Cash."

"Zander Stone, DDPD. Don't recognize the name." They shook hands.

"You wouldn't."

Dixie shrugged out of Zander's hold. "He's from Louisiana, here visiting family."

Zander nodded—as if deciding whether to believe the information or not—and looked the Marine up and down.

Liam stared right back at the officer.

You could cut the tension with a knife.

Dixie rolled her eyes—*silly boys*—and nodded toward the back of the room. "Everyone's over by the fireplace if you want to say hi."

Just then, Zander's phone rang.

"Hang on." He pulled the phone from his pocket. "Stone here... *What?*... You're sure it's her? Where?... *Towering Pines?*... Alright I'm on my way." He clicked off and turned to Dixie. "I gotta go."

Dixie's eyes rounded as she looked at Zander, and understanding her non-verbal question, he nodded—*yes, it's Lizzie.*

Zander spun on his heel, but then stopped, and turned back around. "*Stay here* Dixie. I'm serious."

She flashed him an *are you kidding me* look.

"I'm serious, Dix. I'll let you know when you can come by." And with that, he turned and jogged out the front door.

Dixie met Liam's gaze. She cleared her throat. "Well, it was nice meeting you."

"They found Lizzie, huh?"

She took a deep gulp of her drink and waved to Chuck. "Put this—and his beer—on my tab."

"You got it, Dixie girl."

Dixie turned to Liam and found herself hesitating. Hesitating for what? For him to ask her out? To ask for her number? For him to tell her that he'd fallen madly in love with her during their brief time together? Or, maybe for him to throw her onto the bar and rip her clothes off.

With his eyes locked on hers, he downed his beer and then said, "It was nice meeting you too, Miss Knight. Very nice."

Outside, Zander's police siren silence through the air, shaking her from her haze.

"I gotta go."

He smiled and nodded as she turned and jogged out the front door.

8

$\mathcal{D}$IXIE CRANKED THE heater on high as she navigated the tight corners of the icy mountain road.

The night was as black as coal, and slick as shit.

The unrelenting snow hampered visibility, making an already nerve-wracking drive even more difficult. She flicked the wipers on high and leaned forward, squinting to see through the streaks.

Note to self, get new windshield wipers immediately.

Dixie glanced at the clock—almost ten—and then back at the road. The motel should be close, if her memory served her correctly... which was always a gamble.

What the hell was a girl like Lizzie Meyers doing at the Towering Pines Inn? Meeting John Blevins? Possibly... but a rich, prominent doctor like John Blevins didn't seem the type to book an hour at the seedy motel.

Dixie had only been to the motel twice in her life—once while tailing a suspected jewelry thief, and the second time while investigating an anonymous tip about a national serial killer.

The Towering Pines Inn was not the place to go hang out. Ever.

She wiped the fog from the window as the motel's blinking neon light came into view.

The place was buzzing with activity. Two squad cars, the chief's truck and an ambulance, although, something told Dixie that an ambulance wouldn't be needed... well, maybe for the body bag. A small group of people gathered around a white sports car—Lizzie's, she presumed.

Dixie slowed, contemplating where to park. She knew Zander would give her an ass chewing as soon as he saw her, so she needed to lay low and hang in the shadows for as long as possible.

She pulled into the parking lot and quickly hung a left to avoid being seen. Dixie rolled to a stop under a mass of pine trees, turned off the engine, grabbed her bag, and got out.

Voices and shouts carried through the cold wind, and flashlights bounced off the trees, the snow glittering in the beams of light.

Dixie slipped through the shadows to the building and crept around the corner.

The first thing she noticed were the dark woods surrounding the motel, just feet from the sidewalk. She shook her head—it was almost as though the motel was built to attract misfits.

Zander stood in the doorway of the room on the end, presumably where Lizzie had been found. Chief of Police Mason Moretti paced the sidewalk, barking orders into his cell phone, while another officer roped off the area with yellow police tape.

After taking a moment to consider her options, Dixie

decided to jog around the far side of the building and approach the room from the opposite end.

She turned on her heel and took off, taking note of the ancient-looking security camera above the office—which did *not* point to the motel entry *or* the parking lot. So unless the killer was stupid enough to go into the office, chances were that he, or she, wasn't on tape.

Dixie counted nine rooms as she jogged around the building, only one with a dim light glowing through the window. Out of all the rooms, Lizzie was found in the very last one, tucked deep in the shadows, and Dixie had no doubt that the location was not a coincidence.

She slowed as she came up on the edge of the building, paused and listened.

"...manager said no one was booked in this room. He said that he usually doesn't book the room because of the location. It's not very popular, apparently. He gave me the printout of all the reservations over the last week. No one stayed in this room. Officially, anyway."

"What was the maid doing in the room, then?"

"According to the manager, doing a weekly walk-through."

"We need to find out who—and I mean every single person—that has keys to these rooms. I need their names."

"Yes, sir."

The voices faded and she took her chance.

Dixie slid around the corner, squared her shoulders—confidently, as though she were supposed to be there—and walked to the doorway of the room... and stopped in her tracks.

Her eyes widened as she looked down at the pale, naked body of Lizzie Meyers.

Her stomach rolled.

Blood pooled around Lizzie's head and face, which was

an oozing mush of pulp. Splatters of blood dotted the walls, speckled with hair, skin and skull fragments.

Lizzie Meyers had been bludgeoned to death.

Dixie had been to plenty of gruesome murder scenes, but this one shook her. Maybe it was the sheer violence of it, or maybe it was because Lizzie was a young girl with her whole life ahead of her. Whatever the reason, Dixie had to take a second to swallow the lump in her throat.

An officer breezed past her, without a second glance.

After taking a deep breath, she shoved her emotions aside, and switched to detective mode.

Dixie yanked a pair of blue booties from her bag and slipped them over her boots, and stepped inside. She figured she had about thirty seconds before someone noticed her, so she quickly walked over to the body, kneeled down and began analyzing the scene.

The main blows occurred on the top of Lizzie's head, which meant her attacker had been above her. Her pale face —the side that wasn't beaten to a pulp—was frozen in an unnerving grimace, and her body was squeezed with rigor-mortis, which meant she was, at the most, forty-eight hours deceased. And considering she'd only been declared missing for around twenty-four hours, Dixie guessed her time of death was sometime early in the evening, the night before.

She scanned her skinny, pasty body—no bruises or scratches, which meant no obvious defense wounds. This confirmed what Dixie had already suspected—Lizzie Meyers knew her attacker.

As Dixie's eyes drifted back to the oozing wound on Lizzie's head, she frowned and leaned closer—was something shimmering in her hair? Something sparkling?

Suddenly, noises from the bathroom. Dixie jumped up

and quickly walked outside, pausing at the doorway to take one more look.

No one stayed in this room—those were the words she'd overheard minutes earlier.

If the manager hadn't assigned the room to anyone, then one of two things happened—someone already had the key and obliged themselves to an evening of murder, or someone broke in.

She kneeled down in front of the cheap, wooden door and peered at the knob—a few scratches, but nothing recent. She looked at the latch on the doorframe, squinted, and leaned closer. After a quick glance over her shoulder, she quickly pulled out a cotton swab, swiped the metal, and slipped it into a plastic bag.

"Dammit, *Dixie.*"

Dixie surged to her feet and looked at Zander, who was stepping out of the bathroom with a bag slung over his shoulder, latex gloves on his hands, and booties over his shoes.

"What the hell are you doing here?" He shook his head. "I should've known."

"Not exactly the Four Seasons, is it?"

"No, the Four Seasons has more than one damn security camera." He crossed the room, casually stepping over Lizzie's pale legs. "You can't be here right now. We'll open it up to you later, alright?"

"Is that her car out front?"

He nodded and ushered her outside.

"Anything interesting inside?"

"Not so far. Her purse was in the room, with the wallet still inside."

"So it definitely wasn't a burglary gone wrong."

"Exactly. And no cell phone."

She nodded at the chief—who was very accustomed to the Black Rose team crashing his crimes scenes—and followed Zander to the edge of the woods.

"Murder weapon?"

"The iron lamp."

"Ouch. And he left it?"

"Yep."

"That's bold—he's cocky. Prints?"

"Looking now, but something tells me we aren't that lucky."

"You're looking into the hotel staff?"

"They've already interviewed the manager and got the list of names. We'll run everyone."

"Did the manager, or anyone, know Lizzie?"

"Nope."

She nodded and gazed at the room, which was a buzz of activity. "No defense wounds... and she was naked."

Zander tensed. "Yes, we're doing a rape kit."

"If it were rape, she'd have defense wounds."

"Unless she was drugged."

"True. So either drugged, consensual sex, or, they didn't have sex and maybe just messed around."

He nodded.

"Have you verified John Blevins's whereabouts for last night yet?"

"We just literally found her."

"But you know about the alleged affair, right?"

"Yeah, I'd gotten wind about it."

Nothing was a secret in Devil's Den.

He continued, "We'll be visiting John shortly, and his wife."

"Heard the wife is nuts."

"Nuts is an understatement. Jealous-type, too, or so I hear."

"Interesting. Jealous people do crazy things, no doubt about that." She paused. "I think Lizzie was getting ready for a date, though—before she left her apartment last night."

"What makes you think that?"

Dixie glanced down.

Zander put his hands on his hips. "You went to her place, didn't you?"

She shrugged, and flashed her sweetest, most innocent smile.

"Dammit, Dix." He shook his head. "Okay, what exactly makes you think she was getting ready for a date?"

"Her makeup, clothes, perfume, hair stuff... it was all laid out. I'm telling you, that girl was getting fancied up for something. A date, maybe. Maybe John."

He frowned, in deep thought.

She patted his shoulder. "It's okay, I wouldn't expect a man to pick up on that little detail."

Zander started to open his mouth—to deliver a few obscenities, no doubt—when his phone buzzed. "I gotta take this. I'll call you when you can come back."

"Hey, Zand?"

"What?"

Dixie lowered her voice and stepped forward. "I'll personally cover the cost if you take her body to Graves Laboratory, instead of sending her to the state crime lab."

Zander's eyes narrowed to slits. "So you can get the details from the autopsy first, and solve the case before we do?"

"Come on, you know they'll do it quicker, and with more accuracy. It's a messy case. John Blevins will have nasty lawyers."

He stared at her for a moment, and she knew he was considering it. "I gotta take this call."

Dixie watched him walk away and glanced at her watch —just after eleven. She pulled her keys from her pocket and walked up the sidewalk—nodding as she passed the medical examiner—and stepped onto the parking lot.

She stopped cold. Apparently, she wasn't the only person who had the idea to park under the shadows of the pine trees. Of all the open spots, someone parked right next to her. It was a black, jacked-up Chevy, brand new as far as she could tell.

Dixie freed her right hand—ready to grab her gun if needed—and walked across the dark lot. As she cautiously stepped up to her truck, a chill ran up her spine. From the corner of her eye, a dark figure emerged from the woods. She quickly slid her hand over her gun, spun on her heel, and faced the silhouette, ready for whatever was to come next.

"Sketchy place to park your truck."

Relief washed over her, followed by butterflies tickling her stomach—she knew that voice.

Liam stepped out of the shadows, his tall, muscular body fitting in with the tall pine trees. Snowflakes speckled his dark hair.

She released the grip on her gun. "Good thing I'm not trigger happy."

"Good thing I'm not a murderer—your parking spot says *come get me*."

Dixie relaxed her stance and tried to calm the rush of adrenaline flowing through her—her body's response to simply being in his presence.

"You wouldn't be the first murderer to hang out here in the last few days."

"Found Lizzie, huh?"

She nodded.

"Bludgeoned to death."

She narrowed her eyes and glanced toward the woods. "Doing a little snooping, huh?"

"I have my sources. Any suspects?"

"That's confidential."

He smirked.

Dixie crossed her arms over her chest. "What are you doing out here?"

"Just taking the scenic route home."

She glanced at the snow sliding down his windshield. "Not the best night for a leisurely drive."

"My truck can handle the mountain roads better than yours." He nodded toward her tires. "Your tires are bald, you need to get new ones."

"Do you make it a habit of following women to murder scenes and assessing their vehicles?"

"Only the beautiful ones."

She grinned.

Liam took a step forward, closing the inches between them.

The butterflies tickling her stomach turned into a fluttering flock of seagulls as she looked up, into his dark eyes. He stared down at her with a gaze that sent her heart thudding in her chest. There was an intensity in his eyes that made her senses peak—an intensity that told her he had something on his mind.

"Let me take you to dinner."

Her eyebrows shot up, her eyes rounded. "Are you serious?"

He nodded.

"Liam, I just saw the body of a woman who was beaten

to death. I'm..." she shifted her weight, "I don't have an appetite. And, it's late anyway."

"Tomorrow."

She stared up at him, baffled. Baffled by the moment, his boldness, his confidence, and baffled that she couldn't seem to find her words. She opened her mouth to say something —*anything*—but was silenced when he leaned down, and pressed his lips to hers.

Like a shot of lightning, tingles surged through her body, and her stomach fell to her feet. His lips were full, soft, and commanding as he kissed her—took her.

And left her completely breathless.

Just as her head began to spin, he pulled away, leaving her weak in the knees and bracing the truck behind her.

The snow swirled between them as he looked at her, his eyes rounded, his chest rising and falling heavily. The slight look of surprise on his face faded quickly as the corner of his lip curled up, into a cocky smirk. "Tomorrow, then?"

Dixie blinked—dazed—and shook her head in disbelief of what had just happened.

"Tomorrow, then." Liam turned, got into his truck, and after sending her another smoldering glance, he started the engine and drove out of the parking lot.

She watched his taillights fade into the distance and took a deep breath to calm her racing heart.

What the *hell* just happened?

9

*D*ESPITE THE FRIGID temperature outside, Liam rolled down his window. Tiny snowflakes blew inside as he inhaled the ice-cold air, and shook his head. He was hot as hell and knew it had nothing to do with the heater in his truck, and everything to do with the dark-haired, green-eyed enchantress that he'd just left.

Dixie Knight.

Dixie Knight, Private Investigator.

Dixie Knight, PI, who drove a truck, and carried a gun on her hip.

Jesus Christ.

He didn't know what the hell had come over him when he'd kissed her. Maybe it was the few beers he'd had earlier, or the fact that he hadn't been laid in a month... or maybe it was just her.

Her.

He envisioned her staring up at him under the pine trees —the snow clinging like crystals to her dark, silky hair. Her green eyes seemed to glow in the darkness, reflecting a strength, but also a softness hidden somewhere inside. She was quick-witted, smart, brave—considering her choice of occupation—and independent... and sexy as shit. There was just something about her that was absolutely, completely, irresistible to him.

She'd tasted like vanilla. Her lips were as soft as silk. Her kiss... *the kiss*... was the most amazing kiss he'd ever had in his life.

Liam took a deep breath to ease the raging erection she'd given him.

Dammit, Liam, calm down.

He shook his head again. He couldn't remember a woman working him up like this since... never.

As a special operations Marine, women were as much a part of Liam's life as eating and breathing. They threw themselves at him—not just because he was a Marine, or because of his six-foot-two muscular body and rugged handsomeness, but because Liam carried an air of strength and confidence around him, that brought women to their knees. A subliminal message that said *I'll give you the hottest night of your life, and keep you safe and protected at the same time.*

Not many women could resist Liam Cash. And luckily for them, Liam didn't put up too much of a fight. He'd love them, and leave them, and never give them a second thought.

But then there was Dixie. She hadn't thrown herself at him like most women did—quite the contrary, in fact. But he knew she was interested, or, at the very least, intrigued. There had been an undeniable and immediate connection between them the moment they met eyes across the crowded, country bar.

She was beautiful. The most beautiful woman he'd ever seen in his damn life. And that said a lot. *A lot.*

He'd tried to talk himself out of following her to the

Towering Pines Inn. Sure, he wanted to see her again, but that could have waited. There were two things that pulled him to follow her—his gut instinct that ten years in the Marines taught him never to ignore, and the horrific memories of Terra Voss and Maria Nolen.

Liam plucked his cell phone from the passenger seat.

"Parker here."

"It's Liam, you busy?"

"Just wasting, I mean *working* my life away."

"But still better than boot camp, right?"

"Fuck yeah better than boot camp, man."

Rick Parker, a former Marine and bunkmate of Liam's, had recently accepted a position with the FBI. Eight months ago, Rick was assigned to work a case in Liam's hometown, which Liam had assisted with—off the books, of course.

"I need a favor."

"Anything."

"Can you send me the official files on Terra Voss and Maria Nolen?"

"Terra and Maria? What's going on?" Liam heard the *click, click, click* of a keyboard as Rick began pulling the files.

"They were both young blondes, in their twenties, right?"

"Right."

"Declared missing and then found naked, murdered—beaten to death—in a hotel room, with no signs of struggle, right?"

"Right. It appeared our killer would seduce the women, talk them onto their knees, and then hit them over the head after he got his rocks off. Never found any DNA, or hell, *anything*, of the suspect. The guy's smart, which is why we assumed he never penetrated the victims. Case went cold."

Pause. "What the hell's going on? You're in Devil's Den, on leave, right?"

"Right."

"What's going on, Cash?"

"Just get me those files and I'll be in touch."

Pause. "Alright, buddy. Keep me in the loop, okay?"

"Will do."

Click.

***

The thick clouds masked the early morning sun as Dixie jumped in her truck. There was a break in the snow—*thank God*—but it was just the calm before the storm. Six more inches were expected to fall over the next twelve hours.

She glanced at the clock—seven-forty-five—and picked up her cell phone.

"Stone here."

"Zander, it's Dixie."

"Hey."

"You sound terrible."

"A dead body will do that. Was up all night."

"Did you meet with John Blevins and his wife?"

"Yep." He exhaled and Dixie knew that the sit-down didn't go well.

He continued, "To say Blevins got defensive is an understatement. He's adamant that he and Lizzie were not having an affair, and that he only saw her at the office—never outside of work."

"What about Monday night?"

"Says he saw her during the day, they chatted for a minute, and that was it. Says he went straight home from work, and didn't leave again until the next morning. Offered the security footage from his office."

"No shit?"

"No shit, and we've already reviewed it. He arrived at the office around eight-thirty Monday morning, and we've got him on camera leaving around seven."

"But how do we know he went straight home?"

"Wife says they had dinner, although she couldn't remember the exact time."

"So there's still a window of time unaccounted for. From the time he left the office to the time he arrived home—we don't know that he didn't drive to the Towering Pines to murder Lizzie, before going home for a nice home-cooked meal."

"Right."

"What about pulling his home security footage?"

"There's a little thing called a warrant needed for that, you know that. He's not officially a suspect, so it's delicate."

"As always."

"As always. Anyway, the meeting ended with Suzie screaming in his face, calling him a liar, and storming out of the room. It was awesome."

"Sounds pretty awesome." Dixie chewed on her bottom lip. "Where's Lizzie's body?"

Pause. "I'm working on that."

"Send it to Graves, Zand."

"Working on it." She heard muffled voices in the background. "I gotta go."

"Talk soon."

"Yep."

Click.

Dixie pulled into a narrow parking spot underneath an ice-covered tree. She said a little prayer that a limb wouldn't break and fall on her—or her truck—as she loaded her arms with a tray of coffee, her briefcase, her purse and folders, and finally, started across the parking lot.

The massive, mirrored office building sprawled across the hill ahead of her, sparkling in the streaks of sunlight that burst through the clouds.

Located on the outskirts of Devil's Den, Graves Laboratory was one of the top forensics labs in the country. Privately funded, Dixie's father was the first big investor in the company, which had proven to be invaluable to Black Rose's business. The Knight sisters exclusively used the lab for all of their cases, and were on a first name basis with the staff.

While most evidence from cases handled by the police department went to the state crime lab, the local PD used Graves's services for anything they needed done immediately, for complicated crimes, or high-profile cases that would be under intense scrutiny.

Dixie pushed through the shiny front doors. "Morning, Tom."

The security guard tipped his hat. "Miss Knight."

Carefully balancing her load, Dixie walked across the lobby to April, the busty, red-headed receptionist, who was typing a mile-a-minute across her keyboard. Mesmerized by her speed, Dixie imagined smoke swirling up from the keys. She set the coffee on the counter and flexed her fingers, which were frozen stiff.

The receptionist looked up. "Morning, Dixie! What can I do for you?"

"You can teach me how to type that fast."

April wiggled her fingers and winked. "These fingers are legendary in Devil's Den."

"I'll bet they are." She winked. "I need to see Max."

"Let me see..." Her fingers danced across the keyboard. "He's in meetings all morning."

"Tell him it's me, and I've got a Caramel Macchiato."

April grinned, knowing her boss's weakness for high-dollar coffee. "Okay, hang on." After a few back and forth messages on the computer, she buzzed the door open. "Go on up, Miss Knight."

As the elevator lifted, Dixie glanced at her reflection in the shiny, silver doors. Her cashmere trench-coat had a smear of... something down the arm. Her long, dark hair stuck haphazardly out from the scarf that was wrapped around her neck. Her brown boots were speckled with mud. She was a mess. But it had been a hell of a night of sneaking around Lizzie's murder scene, scoping out John Blevins's home and office, *and* trying to get a certain sexy Marine out of her head. And now, it was just after eight o'clock in the morning and she was running on coffee, and the strawberry jelly-doughnut she'd added to her order at the last minute.

The elevator dinged and the doors slid open.

Dixie was greeted by another young, curvy receptionist —this one, she didn't know.

"Good morning Miss Knight, may I take your coat?" She pushed out of her chair. "Or, your folders, or your coffee..."

"No thanks. I'm here to see Max."

"Yes, right this way."

She followed the tall brunette down a long hallway decorated with expensive paintings. The receptionist knocked on the door at the end of the hall, and cracked it open. "Mr. Blackwood, Miss Knight is here to see you."

Dixie fought an eye-roll as she waited patiently in the hall until Max gave the approval for her to proceed into his luxurious office.

Sheesh.

The brunette turned and smiled. "Go ahead."

"Thanks." She stepped inside as the receptionist closed the door behind her.

"Dixie, how the hell are ya?" Max hung up the phone and pushed out of his chair.

"Who's the new eye-candy?"

He grinned. "Sasha. She's from Russia." He wiggled his eyebrows.

She rolled her eyes. "Geez, could you be more cliché?"

Max Blackwood, former Pathologist turned Forensic Medical Examiner had accepted the role of Director at Graves Laboratories five years ago, and he and Dixie hit it off immediately. In his mid-forties, Max was handsome, straight-shooting, assertive, and one of the smartest men Dixie had ever met. But his intellect only served dead bodies and crime scenes, not women. An eternal bachelor—as he'd been called—Max was as unlucky in love as most of the bodies that lay downstairs in the freezer. Wining and dining he could do all day, but emotions and commitment? Forget about it.

Max eyed the coffee in Dixie's hand as he walked around to the front of his desk.

Dixie smiled and lifted the cup. "One Caramel Macchiato, with extra chocolate drizzle... but only if you help me out."

His hand shot forward. "Done."

She gave him a minute to make love to his coffee as she pulled two evidence bags from her purse, and laid them on the desk.

"Mmm, so good." He licked his lips and looked at the bags. "Okay, what you got?"

"A pink hair tie—need a DNA scan."

"Seriously? I could do that in my sleep."

"Please don't. And, something else too."

He sipped, barely paying her any attention.

Dixie lifted the second evidence bag. "This is a black substance, more like particles, really. I need to know what it is, or whatever information you can pull from it."

"Sounds ominous."

"I found it on the lock of a hotel door."

"The hotel door that held Lizzie Meyers dead body?"

"Bad news travels fast."

"It always does in Devil's Den."

"Do you have the body?"

Max shook his head. "No. I assumed they'd send her to the state crime lab, but I've got a call from the chief that I need to return. He called early this morning."

Dixie hid her smile—Zander came through for her, like he always did. But her offer to cover the cost probably didn't hurt either. "You'll get her soon, it was pretty horrific."

"You on the case?"

"You could say that. I'm checking into a cheating husband who was rumored to have Lizzie as his mistress... and then she turned up dead."

"John Blevins."

"You've heard the rumor?"

"I know everything in this town. He's a son of a bitch. Wouldn't surprise me."

"Wouldn't surprise you if he killed her?"

He paused, shrugged. "That might be a stretch to imagine, but he's an arrogant dick."

"Nice."

"Thanks. What about the wife, Suzie?"

"Not sure with that one..."

"No, I don't see her killing anyone. Too weak." He

sipped. "Where'd you get the hair tie? I'm assuming you think it's Lizzie's?"

She wrinkled her nose and scratched her head. "Do you know ol' Black Magic Balik?"

He shivered. "Yeah..."

"Well, this fell out of her robe. Literally."

"Now *her*, I could see her killing our little Lizzie."

"It doesn't fit... Lizzie was found buck naked, beaten to death in a motel room, twenty miles from her cottage."

"Witches do crazy stuff, Dix. Maybe she put Lizzie under a spell."

"So that she could get her naked and beat her to death?"

He shrugged. "Hey, you never know with a witch. Either way, why would she have one of Lizzie's hair ties?"

"I need you to confirm it's hers first."

He took another long sip, gazing at the evidence bags. "Will do."

"And one more thing, when you get Lizzie's body, take a close look at the hair."

"The hair?"

"Yeah, I swear I saw sparkles, shimmers... or something in her hair."

10

*D*IXIE PULLED INTO the parking lot and braked next to the *Den Care Clinic* sign. She surveyed the area—one car out front, more in the back. Two cameras at the entrance, none on the sides, as far as she could tell.

She slowly drove around to the back of the building—four cars and one shiny, new Porsche in the far corner of the lot. *Bingo.*

She glanced at the back door. One camera, pointed straight ahead. *Perfect.*

After taking a quick look around, Dixie pulled next to the sports car, grabbed a small GPS tracker, and slid out of the passenger side door.

A crow called out from a snow-covered pine tree—announcing the suspicious activity—as she kneeled down and stuck the tracker on the chassis of the car.

She jumped into her truck just as the back door of the clinic opened.

Phew, that was close.

Dixie drove around to the front of the building and parked in *Patient Parking.*

After sliding her recorder—an innocent looking pen—into her coat pocket, she walked up the sidewalk and pushed through the front doors.

The receptionist looked up. "Good morning, how can I help you?"

Dixie glanced at her name tag. "Tanya, is it?"

"Yes ma'am." The receptionist cleared her throat and straightened her tag.

"Tanya, my name is Dixie Knight. Is Dr. Blevins available?"

"Do you have an appointment?"

"Not technically."

Tanya paused—Dixie noticed. "No. I'm sorry, he's booked solid today."

"I only need a few minutes with him. Surely there's a break somewhere."

The receptionist shifted in her seat—something about Dixie made her very, *very* uncomfortable. "No, I'm sorry."

"What about his lunch?"

"Booked."

"I see."

Considering that the gossip was quickly spreading, Dixie wasn't surprised that Dr. Blevins had instructed his staff to deny anyone who wasn't a patient. That was okay though because Tanya, and her nervous tick, had piqued Dixie's interest.

Dixie leaned against the counter. "Do you have a minute to chat?"

"Um, uh," her eyes darted around the empty waiting room, and with no apparent excuse, she nodded. "Sure, a minute I guess." She turned to one of the staff. "Deb, will you watch the front, please?"

Deb frowned, glanced at Dixie, and then nodded. Everyone in the office was on edge.

The door buzzed open and Tanya met her on the other side. "We can go into the conference room."

"Great." Dixie followed her down the hall, searching for Dr. Blevins.

"Would you like some coffee, or water?" Tanya asked as she led Dixie into the conference room.

"No, thanks. Nice office."

Tanya took a seat at the long, shiny table. "Thanks, yeah it is."

Dixie slid into a seat across from her and took a moment to allow the silence to drag out, while assessing the receptionist. Tanya was nervous as hell, and Dixie needed to figure out why.

With long curly, blonde hair and bright blue eyes, Tanya looked like an animated character—an innocent, naïve, animated character. Dixie guessed she was in her mid-twenties, and based on her bare ring finger, was also single.

"Are you from here?"

"No, moved here for this job, a few years ago."

"How do you like it so far?"

"The job, or the town?"

"Both."

"Good. The hours here are good, so that's good."

"Good."

Tanya dropped her hands to her lap, then lifted them back onto the table, and then down to her lap again. "So, um, are you a detective?"

"Private Investigator."

"I thought so. Then, this is about Lizzie?"

Dixie wasn't sure how much information Tanya knew, so

she treaded lightly. "Lizzie came by here frequently, correct? As a pharmaceutical rep?"

Tanya nodded. "Yes, once every week, sometimes every other week."

"Were you two friends?"

"*No.*" The response was immediate, and filled with disdain.

Dixie raised her eyebrows.

Tanya's face began to flush. "I mean... um, no, we only saw each other here at the office."

Dixie narrowed her eyes and cocked her head. "Did you like her?"

"I, um, didn't really know her."

"Did you see her on Monday?"

"Yes, she dropped off some samples."

"What time was that?"

"Around three-thirty in the afternoon."

"Did she leave the samples with you, or go into the back?"

"The back."

"How long was she here, in the office?"

"I'm... um, I'm not sure."

"What time did you leave for the day?"

"Five-thirty."

"Was Dr. Blevins still in the office at that time?"

Pause. "Yes, yes, I think so."

"He drives the Porsche, right?"

She nodded.

"Nice car."

Beads of sweat began to dot Tanya's forehead.

Dixie paused. "Has he ever given you a ride?"

Tanya's mouth dropped open.

"In the car, I mean."

"Oh, um, I can't remember." Her eyes darted across the room.

Dixie leaned forward. "Tanya, were Dr. Blevins and Lizzie Meyers having an affair?"

Just then, the door opened.

"Tanya, we need you up front." Dr. Blevins narrowed his eyes and shot Dixie a *you can go straight to hell* look, before turning back to his receptionist. *"Immediately."*

Tanya shot out of her seat like a bullet and scurried out of the room.

Dixie stood. "Dr. Blevins, I was hoping you had a moment to chat."

His jaw clenched. "I'll bet you were. I've already given my statement to the police, last night. Now if you'll—

"Were you with Lizzie the night she was murdered, Dr. Blevins?"

His cheeks flushed with emotion. "Lizzie and I were nothing more than work acquaintances." He lowered his voice, which was quivering with anger. "I only saw her here, for Christ's sake. And if my wife has hired you to tail me, you're wasting your damn time. Now *get out* of my *fucking* office."

Dixie cocked an eyebrow as Dr. Blevins turned, stomped down the hall, and slammed the door to his office.

She heard whispers in the next room.

She grabbed her purse, stepped into the hall, and after glancing over her shoulder, she quietly stepped to the door and strained to listen.

"...police were there until almost midnight last night. Suzie left and went to a hotel right after..."

Her cell phone dinged.

Shit!

A nurse poked her head out of the room, and looked at Dixie. "Hi, can I help you?"

Dixie fumbled through her purse and silenced her phone. "I'm sorry, I just got turned around. I don't think we've met..."

"Paula Daubs. I'm the head nurse here."

"Dixie Knight, pleasure to meet you. I was just chatting with Tanya in the conference room."

The nurse rolled her eyes. "Geez, did she mess up something else?"

"No, no. I was hoping to get some time with Dr. Blevins today, but it appears that he's all booked up."

The nurse cut a look at the dark-haired, dark-eyed man in an expensive suit, leaning up against a desk in the office. He pushed off the desk and walked to the door. "Dixie Knight?"

"Yes."

"I'm sorry, are you a patient here, or..."

"I'm a private investigator."

The nurse raised her eyebrows.

The man frowned. "I'm Edward Rossi, a friend of John's. Can I help you with something?"

"Sure, do you have a few moments to chat?"

"I was just on my way out, walk with me?"

"Sounds good."

Edward grabbed his coat and briefcase, and after telling Paula to call him if she needed anything, he stepped out of the office.

Dixie fell into step beside him as they walked down the hall. "You mentioned you and John are friends?"

"Yes, for years. I met him in medical school decades ago."

"You're a doctor?"

"Was. Retired. I own this clinic with him. I'm a silent partner."

They pushed out of the front doors and were welcomed by falling snow. She repositioned the recorder pen on her coat.

"So you must know what's going on."

He nodded, his eyes saddening. "Yes, I've heard the rumors."

"Okay then, I'll cut to the chase—were John and Lizzie Meyers romantically involved?"

"No."

"Was he with her Monday night?"

He looked at her. "You're barking up the wrong tree, Miss Knight. John didn't kill her."

"Why are you so sure?"

He stopped, turned. "Why? Because he wouldn't have— he had no reason to. Despite what you've heard, they weren't having an affair." His eyes narrowed. "Despite what Suzie says."

"Why would Suzie think that, then?"

"She thinks he's cheating on her all the time. Jealous type." He blew out a breath. "Look, I was here when Lizzie came by Monday... she seemed upset. Off. Said something about her neighbor..."

"Something about her neighbor? What did she say?"

He squeezed his face. "I'm trying to remember. Oh! Something about how she thinks she saw something that she wasn't supposed to, and then found a dead—mutilated —black cat on her doorstep the next morning. She thinks her creepy neighbor put it there."

"Saw something she wasn't supposed to?"

"Yeah... something like that. Or, maybe someone. Saw *someone* she wasn't supposed to." His phone rang. "I've got to take this." He started to turn, and then turned back. "Dixie, seriously, you're barking up the wrong tree."

Dixie watched him jog across the parking lot, and then pulled out her cell phone.

"Raven here."

"Raven, it's Dixie."

"Oh, good, you've got several messages..."

"Keep them. I need you to look into a few things for me." She started walking to her truck.

"Everything okay?"

"Got a pen? Stupid question. Okay, I need you to pull everything you can on Tanya White. She's the receptionist at Den Care Clinic—John Blevins's clinic."

"Suspect?"

"Something's definitely going on there. Whether she knows something, or had a part in something, I don't know, but she was shaking like a Chihuahua the entire time we spoke. She got all worked up talking about John, and she's definitely not a fan of Lizzie Meyers. The girl knows something."

"All worked up? Could *she* be having an affair with John?"

"Not sure, but if so, that guy must have a golden penis or something."

"Golden penis? What was his phone number again?"

Dixie smirked. "You need a boyfriend. Anyway, she was holding back, no doubt about it. I also need you to pull a list of every employee in the clinic, past and present. Anyone who might've had contact with Lizzie."

"Got it. Anything else?"

"Yeah... I need to know more about Black Magic Balik. We need to know where she was Monday night. Have Ace see if he can pin her location for that night."

"Will do. Are you coming in?"

"Nope, I'm going to visit the neurotic wife."

"Ask about the golden penis."

"I'll lead with that."

"Have fun."

Click.

11

*D*IXIE CLICKED ON her recorder as she walked down the long hallway that led to the penthouse suite.

According to the desk clerk—who was more than willing to provide details of Suzie Blevins's stay for a free cup of coffee—Suzie stormed into the hotel around one in the morning, with her dogs in tow, and demanded the best room available, and two bottles of wine. Bordeaux, apparently.

As Dixie reached the suite, she took a deep breath and said a little prayer that Suzie's reputation for being a nutcase wasn't true, and that the meeting would be productive.

The moment her knuckle tapped the door, wild barking —yapping—ensued from the room.

After a muffled, *"Shut up!"*, the door swung open. Dressed in a silk robe, pink slippers, and diamond earrings, Suzie looked Dixie up and down.

"Mrs. Blevins..."

"Suzie."

"Okay, Suzie, I'm Dixie Knight."

Suzie's eyes widened, and her face softened minimally—as much as it could around the fillers, of course.

"*Oh.* Come in."

She stepped inside and looked around the spacious suite. An empty bottle of wine lay in the middle of the seating area, which was centered in front of sweeping windows that overlooked the snow-covered mountains. She glanced at the kitchen and bar—more empty wine bottles. A few dark spots speckled the plush carpet, presumably a gift for the staff from Suzie's precious miniature poodles.

Suzie swatted at her dogs, demanding their silence, and closed the door. "I'm sorry I haven't returned your call... It's been a shitty twenty-four hours. Anyway, I've heard so much about you, but we've never met."

"It's a pleasure. Do you have a few minutes to chat?"

"Yes." She walked across the room. "Would you like a drink?"

"No, thank you."

"Alright then, I'll have one for both of us." She plucked a bottle off the counter and poured a glass. "I'm assuming you've spoken with my lawyer, Hank?"

"Yes, yesterday."

"I told him to tell you that I'll pay whatever. Initially, I just wanted you to catch the cheating son of a bitch so I could kick his ass to the curb, but now that his little mistress is dead, I need you to prove he did it." She walked to the sitting area and sank into the white leather couch.

Dixie sat across from her. "My job isn't to prove that he did or didn't do it, but to gather evidence, either way."

"Whatever, same thing."

Actually, not at all, but she didn't want to argue semantics.

"Suzie, what makes you think your husband was cheating on you?"

"What doesn't?" She sighed. "First, he has before—three times—and I've caught him every time." She sighed. "It's always the same thing... getting late night texts, long meetings after work, he gets in the shower immediately when he gets home. All the classic signs. Anyway, I let the three before slide, but now, I've had it. I'm done with him."

"When did the signs begin?"

"A few months ago."

Dixie scribbled on her notepad. "What makes you think he was cheating with Lizzie Meyers, specifically?"

Suzie pushed off the couch and began pacing. "That blonde bitch would go see him every week, sometimes twice."

"Well, she was a pharmaceutical sales rep... that was her job."

"Was it her job to stay in his clinic after hours?"

Dixie raised her eyebrows. "When did you see this?"

"Twice. It was late at night, and John still wasn't home, so I drove by the clinic and her little white sports car was out front."

"What time?"

"Past ten at night, both times."

Interesting.

"Did you see John there?"

"He always parks in the back, and I didn't want to pull in. But he wasn't home, so where else would he have been?"

"Did you check his phone?"

"He keeps it locked—with a code I don't know, of course." Her face squeezed with anger as she gazed out the window and muttered, *"Cheating son of a bitch."*

Dixie paused. "Do you think your husband would kill

Lizzie?"

Suzie's head snapped toward Dixie. "No doubt in my mind."

"Why?"

"I just do."

"Has he ever been physical with you?"

"Kicked the dogs before."

Being on the receiving end of Suzie's dogs' welcome, that wasn't a stretch to imagine. But kicking a dog doesn't exactly make him a murderer—asshole, yes, but murderer, no.

"Has he ever put his hands on you?"

"No, he knows I'd kick his ass."

"Okay, so if he did it, what's the motive? Why would he kill Lizzie?"

Suzie sipped—taking a moment to choose her words carefully. "Maybe he knew I'd hired you—he knew he was going to get caught and the little blonde bitch would admit to everything. He knew I'd leave him this time." She narrowed her eyes. "And, Miss Knight, he knew I would bleed him for every single penny he has." Pause. "Money makes people do crazy things, you know."

Dixie nodded—in her line of work, she'd seen the poisoning effect money had on people and how it changed them to the very core. The desperation, the greed, the obsession.

A moment of silence dragged out. Dixie leaned forward. She had another angle she needed to explore—delicately.

"Let's go back to Monday night. Did your husband come home right after work?"

"Yes, well, he got home around seven, I think, and we had dinner." Suzie sat down and coaxed her quivering poodle onto her lap.

"And what did you do after dinner?"

"I went upstairs and took a long bath. I fell asleep in the tub, and when I woke up, I got into bed."

Fell asleep, or passed out?

"You didn't go anywhere after dinner?"

"No."

"Didn't leave the house at all?"

"No."

"And you didn't see or communicate with your husband after dinner?"

"No."

"So, really, he could've gone somewhere."

"Yes."

And, so could've you.

"Did you speak with anyone—call, text, anything, that night?"

"No." She cocked her head. "Why are you asking me this?" Suddenly, her pointy eyebrows shot up. "Unless you're checking to see if *I* have an alibi for Monday night."

"I'm just being thorough, ma'am."

Suzie surged to her feet, sending her poodle tumbling to the floor, and sloshing wine on the couch. "I'm sure as hell not paying you to interrogate *me*, Miss Knight."

"This is hardly an interrogation, Mrs. Blevins."

"I *said* to call me Suzie—I hate that last name."

The dog whimpered at Suzie's feet as she glowered at Dixie. "I don't have time for this bullshit." She stomped to the front door and yanked it open. "Miss Knight, you have twenty-four hours to prove that my husband killed Lizzie Meyers. If not, I fire you and keep the deposit."

Dixie calmly raised off the chair and walked to the door. With barely a smile—*a smug smile*—she said, "It was such a pleasure meeting you, Mrs. Blevins."

And with that, the door slammed behind her.

*I*T WAS ALMOST six o'clock as Dixie turned onto the long, icy driveway of Black Rose Investigations.

Stan the weatherman was right—it had snowed all day, which made for a hell of an afternoon staking out Dr. Blevins, his wife, and Black Magic Balik, as well as doing surveillance for a few other cases she was working on. Dr. Blevins never left his office, Suzie stayed in her penthouse suite, and not surprisingly considering the weather, the witch didn't step foot outside, not even to feed the four black cats that roamed the grounds.

Edward Rossi's story about the dead cat on Lizzie's doorstep the morning she went missing didn't sit well with Dixie—it certainly had Balik's name written all over it. On the other hand, maybe the cat was sick, or attacked by an animal, and just so happened to die on Lizzie's doorstep... or maybe the story wasn't true at all.

She pulled around to the back of the house, sliding on a patch of ice before finally coming to a stop.

Damn bald tires.

She grabbed her purse, briefcase, her folders and jogged to the back door. After wiping her boots on the *Go Away* mat, she stepped inside.

"Hey, Dixie."

"Hey, Raven. What're you still doing here?"

"Wrapping up a few things. Need some help?" She grabbed the folders from Dixie's hands.

"Thanks." She shimmied out of her coat and hung it up. "It's really coming down out there."

"Hell of a day for stalking people."

"Tell me about it. I've drank, like, six cups of coffee today —mainly to stay warm."

"How was the wife?"

"Suzie?" Dixie started toward her office, with Raven at her side. "Not quite as crazy as everyone says she is, but a pistol, no doubt about it. Hates her husband. Hates Lizzie even more."

"Enough to kill her?"

"She says she was home Monday night and didn't leave the house." She cut Raven a glance. "But has no alibi."

"And, neither does he, right?"

"Right."

Dixie flicked on her office light, tossed her purse on the floor and sank into her chair. "What did you dig up on John's receptionist, Tanya White?"

Raven glanced down at her notebook. "Twenty-four, former college cheerleader, majored in Communications, loves cats and hates seafood. Dropped out of college, moved back in with her parents, a few towns over, and couldn't find a job until she came across the help wanted ad for John's clinic. Got the job and moved here. She rents a cute little house on the lake, not too far from here actually."

"On the lake, huh?"

"Yep, boat dock and everything."

"Boyfriends?"

"No, she bitches about being single on social media, but she did recently post a comment about older men and how they really know how to handle themselves—sexual innuendo written all over it."

"Older men?" Dixie leaned back. "Interesting."

"Thought so too." She tossed a piece of paper on the desk. "Here's the printout of all the employees at Den Care Clinic, past and present."

"Perfect, thanks, Rave."

The phone rang.

"No problem." She stood. "We'll be at the Black Crow later if you want to meet up."

"We'll see." Dixie picked up the phone as Raven walked out of the office.

"Dixie here."

"Dix, it's Max."

"Did you get Lizzie's body?"

"Yep, early this morning, right after you left. That's why I'm calling."

Her stomach did a little dance. "Okay..."

"You've got one hell of an eye, Eagle Eye."

"Don't call me that. Keep going..."

"Tess has been working on the autopsy all afternoon, and we've found something interesting already."

"Yeah?"

"Yeah. Lizzie Meyers has tiny specks of gold in her hair."

"Gold? Like, *real* gold?"

"*Real* gold. That must've been the sparkle you noticed, Eagle Eye."

Dixie frowned and shook her head. "Are you sure?"

"Don't insult me."

"Could it be from a headband or something?"

"No, it's mainly only around the point of impact on her head—that's what strikes me as odd."

"Only around the wound? Where she was hit?"

"Right."

"Anywhere else on her body?"

"Some on her hands and arms, but mainly on the head."

"What about her clothes?"

"Nope... which makes me think that whatever it is got on her *after* she was undressed."

"What the *hell*? Could it be from jewelry? Breaking during the beating or something?"

"No, these are tiny, tiny, almost microscopic specks of gold."

Pause. "Zander said she was beaten with a lamp..."

"Already called—not that I needed to, I was pretty sure that the Towering Pines Inn didn't have golden lamps—and I was right, they don't."

"Son of a bitch."

"My thoughts exactly."

"What about the rape kit?"

"She wasn't penetrated, but Tess isn't completely done looking her over yet. I'll forward you the full autopsy report once it's complete."

"Thanks."

"And one more thing, I scanned that black shit you pulled from the door lock. It's iron-based magnetic particles."

"What's—

"From a credit card—the black stripe on a credit card."

Dixie nodded. "Ah, so exactly what I thought... our killer broke into the hotel room. Using a credit card."

"That would be my assumption."

"Well, we can cross off the motel staff from the list now. Can you tell anything else from it?"

Boisterous laughter rang out from the other end of the phone. "You mean, can I read the credit card number, the name, and address of the person who broke into the room and killed Lizzie Meyers? No, Dix, sorry."

She rolled her eyes. "Smartass. Okay, thanks for the info and call me with anything else."

"Will do."

Click.

As she hung up, Raven gingerly stepped into the doorway, with a grin plastered across her face. "Um, Miss Knight, there's someone here to see you."

Dixie cocked her head as Raven stepped aside, and Liam's tall, muscular body filled the doorframe.

Her breath caught.

His eyes locked on hers and the corner of his lip curled up.

She cut Raven a glance, who was still grinning from ear to ear.

"Can I come in?" His voice was smooth, deep and so, so sexy.

Insecurity shot through her as she looked around her messy office. She stood, to clean off a chair, and felt another twinge of insecurity when she remembered she hadn't even glanced in a mirror since the morning.

Why the hell did this guy have such an impact on her?

"Sure, yes, come on in."

He stepped into the room and her pulse picked up.

"I wasn't sure if you'd still be here."

Dixie walked around her desk and pulled the folders and candy wrappers from one of the chairs. "I just got in, actually."

"Been in a ditch all day?"

She smirked. "I plan to get new tires next week, thank you very much."

"Good."

He smiled and her eyes trailed down to his full, succulent lips. The lips that had passionately caressed hers underneath the pine trees the night before. Her cheeks began to flush.

She felt his eyes on her backside as she turned and slid the folders on the file cabinet and tossed the candy wrappers in the trash. "Sorry, I haven't had time to clean up around here."

Raven snickered from the hallway.

"Busy with PI stuff?"

"Yes, *PI stuff.*"

Liam sat down, kicked out his legs, and she had to fight herself from looking at his thick thighs.

"So the motel room was broken into?"

Dixie leaned against the desk, in front of him, and crossed her arms over her chest. "Eavesdropper."

"My ears are trained to listen." The playfulness faded from his eyes. "Have they made any arrests?"

"No, not yet."

"Any leads at all?"

"A few..."

"But nothing concrete."

"Right." She paused. There was a total shift in him all of the sudden, in his demeanor. "What's going on?"

He stared at her for a moment, and then leaned forward. "I've been thinking... why don't you leave this case to the police?"

"What? Why would I do that?"

"I just think they're better equipped to handle it."

"So you stopped by to insult me?"

"No, to take you to dinner, remember?"

"Why do I have a feeling there's a little more to this visit than that? Why do you want me to drop the Lizzie Meyers case?"

Pause. "It's dangerous, Dixie."

Dixie pushed off the desk and stared down at him. He was protective of her—she saw it under the pine trees the night before, and she saw it in his eyes, now.

"Why don't you tell me what's going on, Liam?"

Liam glanced over his shoulder before turning back to her, and she knew that whatever he was about to tell her was going to change the course of her investigation.

He stood, towering over her, and pulled a piece of paper from his pocket.

"I think Lizzie Meyers's death is connected to two murders in my hometown in Louisiana, about eight months ago."

She raised her eyebrows. "Why?"

He handed her the piece of paper. "Both girls, Terra Voss and Maria Nolen, were found naked—signs of sexual activity, but never penetrated—bludgeoned to death, beaten by a single object on the top of the head."

Her eyes widened.

Liam continued, "Both girls were young—mid-twenties —and blonde. They resembled each other... and they both resemble Lizzie Meyers."

Dixie opened the piece of paper with the details. "Any suspects?"

"No. The case went cold."

A chill ran up her spine. "Do you have the autopsies?"

"I've got their full files."

"I need to see those files."

"To check if they had gold specks in their hair?"

Her mouth fell open. "Did they?"

His eyes darkened. "Yes."

"Oh, my God."

Liam began pacing. "The FBI got involved. This case is personal to me, I helped out on it." He plucked the paper from her hands. "You need to leave this case alone, Dixie. Leave it to the authorities."

Dixie's phone rang. As her mind raced with this new information, she reached over and picked it up.

"Dixie here."

"Hey, it's Roxy," her sister said in a whisper. "I'm at the police station working a case and I overheard a call that just came in. Another girl has been found beaten to death—top of the head. Fresh, apparently, within the last hour. The neighbor was dropping by some mail and saw her through the window."

"*What?*"

"She was found just this second. If you hurry, you can check out the scene before anyone gets there. It's a lake house—39 Shore Road."

Her stomach rolled. "Did you say a lake house?"

"Yeah, some girl named Tanya."

Tanya White.

13

*D*IXIE SET DOWN the phone and looked at Liam. "Another one?"

"Another one." She grabbed her purse. "I gotta go."

Liam stepped in front of her. "I'm going with you."

"No, you're not."

"The roads are covered, especially to the lake." He glanced at the snow falling heavily outside. "My truck will get us there twice as fast."

Shit. Damn bald tires.

Her mind raced. "Wait... I've got another idea. Let's go."

"I'll go start the truck."

Dixie nodded and began gathering her things.

***

Liam pulled his cell phone from his pocket as he jogged outside.

"Rick here."

"Rick, it's Liam." He jumped in his truck, and opened the piece of paper he'd swiped from Dixie's desk. "I need you to run a list of names for me. See if anything pops up."

"What is it?"

"A list of employees at Den Care Clinic."

"Why the hell..." Pause. "This wouldn't happen to do with Terra and Maria, would it?"

No response.

"Liam, if you've got a lead, you need to tell us. The FBI took over the case. You're in over your head, man."

"Just scan the names and we'll go from there."

Pause. "Alright."

"I'm sending a picture of the paper now."

"Talk soon."

Click.

***

Dixie jumped in the passenger seat, and Liam started the engine.

"Where to?"

"The docks. About two miles from here."

He shoved the truck in drive and gunned it down the driveway.

The sun had just set, and the blue glow of twilight washed over the snow-covered mountains. And, Liam was right—the roads were completely covered.

She yanked her phone from her purse.

He glanced over. "What are you doing?"

"Checking something."

"Checking what?"

"I put a tracker on John Blevins's car this morning. Let's see if he made a trip to the lake in the last hour." A minute slid by as she worked her cell phone. "*Dammit.* He's still at the office and hasn't left."

"So your prime suspect wasn't anywhere in the vicinity."

"Right." She shook her head as frustration began to

bubble up. "I was *just* with Tanya, this morning—not seven hours ago. I can't believe this." She leaned forward and squinted to see through the snow. "Turn here."

He drove past the sign for Devil's Lake and parked beside the docks. Dozens of boats swayed lazily in the black water.

"Which one's yours?"

"The one on the end. Let's go."

They jogged to the last dock, and Dixie jumped in as Liam untied the boat.

"Gonna be cold."

He shot her a *give me a break* look.

She inserted the key and after a few sputters, the boat came to life, sending black smoke swirling into the cold wind.

Liam joined her up front. "Nice boat."

"Thanks. It was my dad's, he was a ski fanatic."

She carefully maneuvered away from the dock and sped into the night. The last of the day's light sat on the lake's horizon, fading into deep indigo where the stars were just beginning to twinkle. It would be completely dark in ten minutes.

The frigid air sliced through her hair as the boat bumped over the waves.

"How far to the lake house?"

"Five minutes. Would've been thirty, probably, if we took the roads."

"So we've got less than twenty minutes before the cops show up."

She glanced at him. "Exactly."

What seemed like seconds later, Dixie slowed and navigated the boat to a small dock, jetting out from the woods.

"I think this is it."

Liam jumped out and secured the boat while Dixie grabbed her bag and looked around—it was a steep climb to the house, which was going to be even more difficult because of the snow and ice.

Liam joined her as she stepped off the dock. She sensed a shift in him—he'd switched to Marine mode the second they'd stepped out of the boat. A determined, alert, take-no-prisoners soldier with laser focus.

"Let's go."

As they climbed the steep terrain, she felt Liam close behind her, ready to catch her if she fell—protective, once again.

They emerged from the tree line and stepped onto the back lawn. Darkness had fallen.

Dixie pulled the flashlight from her bag and Liam grabbed her arm.

"No. Keep the light off for now. Whoever did this could still be here. I want you to get behind me, stay behind me, and don't leave my side." He looked down at her, his eyes fierce. "Do you understand?"

Something in her gut twisted. She nodded.

Liam reached into his jacket and pulled out his gun. "Let's go."

She stayed on his heels as they darted across the yard, under the cover of shadows. The sound of the water lapping against the dock faded into the distance, and was replaced by the whistle of the wind sweeping through the trees.

They crept up the side of the house, and finally, to the front porch.

"Wait." Dixie whispered as she grabbed his arm. "Put these on." She pulled two pairs of booties and gloves from her bag. "We can't contaminate the crime scene, or leave your prints."

He nodded and slipped them on.

Gun raised, he stepped onto the porch, scanned the surroundings, and then nodded for her to come up.

Dixie pulled on her gloves and booties, stepped up, and took inventory—a single rocking chair, two empty flower pots, a bag of trash, and a large window with a view inside the house, which appeared to be dark.

From first glance, there were no apparent signs of a break-in. Was it possible that Tanya knew her killer? Just like Lizzie appeared to?

She tried the doorknob—unlocked. She turned toward Liam as she clicked on her flashlight.

He shook his head. "I go first."

She nodded and moved aside, and he slowly stepped over the threshold. Her heart started to race as he disappeared into the dark house. The seconds seemed like hours, until finally, he emerged from the darkness and motioned her inside.

The moment she stepped into the house, her stomach sank—the smell of fresh blood hung like a wet blanket in the air.

She raised her flashlight and slowly scanned the floor—until the beam landed on the naked, motionless body of Tanya White. Just outside of the massive puddle of blood that encircled her head, lay an iron fire-poker, with chunks of blonde hair stuck to it.

Dixie's hand began to tremble.

Suddenly, in the distance, sirens wailed.

Her head snapped toward Liam, who was staring at the body on the floor. "We gotta go."

He didn't move.

She grabbed his arm. "Liam, we've got to go."

He looked at her, with a fire in his eyes that sent a chill up her spine.

She grabbed his hand and tugged him outside where blue and red lights flashed off the trees.

As Liam closed the door, Dixie paused, grabbed the bag of trash, and then jumped off the porch.

14

*D*IXIE JUMPED INTO the boat and started the engine as Liam untied it from the dock.

"Come on, Liam!"

Car doors slammed in the distance as he jumped in, and they sped off.

Her heart pounded in her chest and despite the cold wind, sweat beaded under her sweater. She felt lightheaded, dizzy.

She felt like she couldn't breathe.

As they neared the center of the lake, she slowed down, and felt Liam's steady gaze on her.

"You okay?"

Dixie took her hands off the wheel, which were shaking with adrenaline, and took a deep breath.

"Yeah, sorry. It's just... I'd just... I'd literally just spoken to her this morning and now she's dead. I can't help but think..." Her eyes burned with tears. "What if I had something to do with it?"

The boat slowed to a stop in the middle of the lake. Snowflakes swirled around them. It was pitch-black except for the glow of the dashboard behind the steering wheel.

Liam stepped closer to her, and turned her toward him. "Dixie, listen to me. You did *not* cause this, okay? This is *not* your fault."

She inhaled, trying to control the emotions flooding her system.

"Come here." He pulled her to him, and wrapped his arms around her.

He was warm, strong—a surprising safe-zone among so much chaos. So much death and chaos.

He squeezed her tighter as the boat lightly rocked back and forth in the black water.

His hand softly stroked her hair, and she squeezed her eyes shut and took another deep breath, inhaling the scent of his skin.

"You're freezing." Liam slid out of his jacket and placed it around her shoulders, pulling her even closer.

She looked up, into his whiskey brown eyes.

Butterflies fluttered in her stomach as he looked down at her—a different kind of intensity shining from his eyes now. A hunger. A look that sent goosebumps across her body—a look that told her she was in trouble.

His eyes drifted to her lips.

Her heart started to race.

Then, he leaned down and kissed her, his warm lips sliding over hers, his grip around her tightening.

He dropped his jacket from her shoulders and took her face in his hands, commanding her submission to him, kissing her like his life depended on it. He was in control, and it made her melt.

Dixie's knees weakened, shivers ran across her skin. Her entire body responded to him, and an uncontrollable need for him overcame her. She let go of all the thoughts racing through her head, and as if her hands had a mind of their own, she tugged off his shirt.

Her coat slid to the floor, her sweater was pulled from her body. Her heart skipped a beat as he unhooked her bra.

The cold air felt invigorating against her heated skin.

Dixie's breath caught as he squeezed her breasts, before grabbing her bare waist and lifting her off the boat, making her feel as though she weighed ten pounds. She wrapped her legs around him, her nipples rubbing against his chest, and kissed him madly as he carried her to the back.

He laid her on the padded deck, then yanked off her boots, her jeans, her silk panties—the aggressiveness driving her crazy. The cold wind swept over her skin as she watched him gaze down at her naked body, his chest rising and falling heavily. He kicked off his boots, tugged off his jeans, and slid out of his boxers. The dim light of the boat glowed around him, outlining his massive body. The sheer size of him would be terrifying in any other situation. With his eyes locked on hers, he crawled on top of her.

His muscular body hovered over her, and for a moment, he just stared at her, making her stomach flip-flop, before crushing his lips against hers.

His erection dangled above her bare stomach and she had to fight from taking a peek. The wet tip swept over her abdomen before he lowered further down.

A hand slid between her legs.

Liam took her nipple into his mouth, nipped, and then sucked, while his fingertips traced her inner lips below. Her body flushed wet with desire. She widened her legs for him, aching for him to touch her sweet spot.

His tongue slid up her neck, and as he licked her ear, his

finger lightly ran over her clit, sending a jolt of electricity through her system. She groaned and tipped her head back as he began to rub tiny circles over her throbbing, swollen bud.

The heat rose between her legs, the tingles intensifying on her delicate skin.

He dipped his fingers deep inside her, and then glided his wet fingertips over her, again. Slowly, lightly, rubbing at first, and then faster and faster.

The tingling turned into a throbbing—every muscle in her body began to tense.

"Oh, Liam..."

The sensation peaked and she arched her back as the orgasm ripped through her—a wave, over and over again.

Finally, it stopped, and she opened her eyes, blinking away the disorientation.

Liam stared down at her with a small smile on his lips, soaking in every second of her euphoria.

"Wow..." She said in barely a whisper.

Something sparked in his eye. "We're not done."

She bit her lip as he nuzzled into her neck and whispered in her ear, "Are you ready?"

"Yes."

Dixie widened her legs and tensed, feeling the sweet twinge of pain as he slid inside her.

He pressed deep, paused, and in a breathy whisper said, "Oh my *God*, Dixie."

She wrapped her legs around him, thrusting her hips forward—giving him exactly what he wanted, which was every inch of her. She squeezed around him as he slid out, and glided back in.

Goosebumps spread across her skin as they seamlessly moved together, with the soft rocking of the boat.

His breath became heavy against her neck, his grip around her tightening.

He pushed deeper, sliding in and out of her wetness.

She dug her fingernails into his back.

"Oh, Liam..."

He thrust harder, faster—her clit throbbing against the friction of his skin.

"*Liam.*" She screamed his name as her body released, for the second time.

"*Dixie,*" he said at the same time, as his body tensed and he poured everything he had into her.

He collapsed on top of her, sweaty, breathing heavily, and kissed her forehead before rolling off.

Tiny snowflakes danced down from the dark sky as they lay next to each other.

Liam turned and looked at her.

Dixie met his gaze, and for a moment, they stared at each other, a nonverbal understanding of what had just happened between them—not just the mind-blowing sex, but the connection, the chemistry, the raw passion that had sent fireworks exploding through their heads.

15

*I*T WAS JUST past eight o'clock by the time they arrived back at Black Rose. The snow had picked up, nearly doubling the time it took to get back to the office. It was a winter whiteout.

As Dixie grabbed the door handle, Liam put his hand on her arm. She turned, looked at him—and somehow, he was even more attractive to her now.

He leaned forward and kissed her softly on the lips, lingering for a moment before pulling away.

She smiled.

Her body felt calm, loose, content. Her brain, like mush. Her heart, a steady beating with desire for the man who'd held her, made her feel safe, and had given her the most incredible, earth-shattering sex she'd ever had in her life.

Liam smiled and turned off the engine.

Dixie watched him unfold from the driver's seat—her gaze trailing down to his perfect backside—before taking a deep breath to compose herself, and getting out. She grabbed the trash bag she'd swiped from Tanya's front porch, and met Liam at the back door.

"Anyone still here?"

"I'm sure. We're kind of a twenty-four-hour office around here." She set the bag of trash on the patio and pushed open the door.

It was quiet, still. Not even Ace's television—that he always kept on—blared from upstairs.

Liam looked around the large kitchen. "You know, this place isn't that creepy. It's beautiful, actually."

She tossed her purse on the table and smiled. "Thanks, I think so too. It's perfect for us."

He helped her out of her jacket, lightly grabbed her shoulders and turned her to face him.

Butterflies, again.

He smiled a soft smile, lightly touched her cheek, and kissed her, again.

"I just had to do that one more time."

Feeling weightless, she opened her eyes and whispered, "One more."

He kissed her again.

She smiled and pulled back. "Okay, now we have to get to work."

"Digging through the trash?"

"Yep."

He wrinkled his nose.

"I'm feeling lucky. The fact that it was sitting on the porch makes me think she had just set it out."

He cocked his head.

"A little PI lesson—someone's trash is a treasure trove of information. You wouldn't believe what you can tell about someone from their trash... maybe something will lead me to whoever killed her."

"Okay, you have fun with that. I've got a few calls to

make." He paused. "How about I grab something for dinner before the town shuts down?"

She started to protest, but realized she hadn't eaten a thing since lunchtime.

"Food sounds good, actually."

"Good. I'll be back with dinner soon."

He kissed her again, and this time, pulled her to him and lifted her off her feet.

***

Liam climbed into his truck, started the engine, and pulled his phone from the console.

"You've reached Rick Parker, FBI, leave a message."

"Parker, it's Liam. There's been an escalation since we last spoke. I need you to run that list of names I gave you—the employees at Den Care Clinic, ASAP." He paused. "I think Terra and Maria's killer is here in Devil's Den... I'll give you the details as soon as you call me back, but I want you to dispatch a team out here immediately. Tonight. Call me back."

He clicked off the phone and blew out a breath.

He had no doubt Dixie would be pissed as hell at him if she found out he informed the FBI of Lizzie and Tanya's murders—they'd swoop in and take over, and she'd lose her case.

But he didn't care.

From the moment he laid eyes on Dixie, he knew he had to have her—as his, as his own. His gut told him she wasn't like anyone else, that she was something special. And the last hour had proven his instinct was right—he'd never, in his life, felt so connected to someone, so quickly.

And hell on earth wasn't going to take that away from him. He couldn't risk her getting caught in the crosshairs of a brutal serial killer.

Now he just had to figure out how to distract her, and keep her occupied until the FBI got to town.

**

Dixie kneeled down and carefully laid the garbage bag on its side.

"Wait, Dix, tarp first." Raven pushed through the back door. "Wow, the snow has really picked up."

Dixie looked up, surprised. "Hey. I didn't know you were still here."

"I was in my office. I was going to come out when I heard the door open, but I saw you had company—a six-foot-two hunk of sexy man-candy." She winked. "So I stayed quiet."

Dixie felt the heat rise to her cheeks.

Raven grinned. "Are we enjoying this man-candy?"

Dixie exhaled, surprised at the sudden rush of emotions. "He's only here for *two weeks*, Rave."

"That's perfect for you then, right? No strings attached. Just have fun."

Dixie glanced down. Normally, that would be perfect for her—she could have fun with her new toy, or *man-candy* as Raven called him, and then say goodbye, never having to get emotionally attached.

The problem was, she already felt attached—very attached.

She shook her head and changed the subject. "It's freezing out here. Go yell at Ace, tell him to bring out two of those portable heaters."

"Good call." Raven stood, brushed off her pants, and yelled at Ace through the door. She kneeled back down and pulled on a pair of latex gloves.

"Here we go."

Dixie sliced the trash bag down the center, and to her relief, it wasn't as stinky as most. "Lucked out here."

Raven nodded enthusiastically. "Hell yeah we did. Remember Bart Labonsky's trash?"

Dixie wrinkled her nose. "How could I forget? That man had to have eaten three cans of sardines a day."

Raven squeezed her face and shook her head. "*Sooo* nasty."

Dixie leaned forward and began poking through. "Okay, so Tanya liked bananas, frozen dinners... *gross*, she was on her period... ah, here's an electric bill." She pulled out the piece of paper. "Late notice. Our girl was low on cash."

"Here's another. Late on the cable bill, too."

"Yikes." Dixie poked around some more, and plucked out a piece of bright silver foil. "What's this?"

Raven leaned forward. "Chateaux LaRouse?"

Dixie's eyebrows shot up. "We're looking at the label of a four-hundred-dollar bottle of Champagne."

"No shit?"

"No shit."

"It was on top too, so she'd just thrown it away."

"I don't see the bottle."

"Recycle bin probably."

Dixie nodded.

"Considering the late bills, where would Tanya get the money to buy a four-hundred-dollar bottle of Champagne?"

Dixie sat back on her heels. "She didn't. Our perp did."

"Huh?"

"Whoever beat her to death." She paused, in deep thought. "Our killer brought the Champagne."

Just then, her cell phone rang.

"Dixie here."

"Dix, it's Max. They brought us Tanya White's body an hour ago and we dove right in. Guess what we found in her hair?"

"Bullshit."

"No, not bullshit."

"Don't tell me—the gold specks."

"Bingo."

Goosebumps prickled her skin. It was the first piece of real evidence linking the two bodies to the same murderer, and, potentially to the two additional murders in Liam's hometown.

Four women, bludgeoned to death, with mysterious specks of gold found in their hair—four women's lives cut short by a merciless killer.

She shook her head, processing the information.

"Also, the pink hair tie that you got from Black Magic Balik—it's Lizzie's."

"You're sure?"

"You've hit me with two of those insults in the last twenty-four hours. Yes, I'm sure, I'm always sure. Her hair was wrapped around it. Solid DNA."

"So... gold specks on both bodies, and a witch hoarding one of the victim's hair ties."

"I told you, voodoo... and maybe a little fairy dust to go along with that."

She glanced toward the dark woods, her mind reeling.

"That's all I have for you right now, will call when I get more info."

"Thanks, Max."

Click.

Dixie shoved her phone into her pocket as Raven carefully pushed a used tissue to the side.

She stood, contemplated.

Raven cocked her head. "What's going on?"

"I've got to go check something out. Will you have Ace pull the orders from Banshee's Brew liquor store for that brand of Champagne? Someone special-ordered it, they don't keep that on the shelves. Have him check for John and Suzie Blevins, and Marden Balik, specifically."

"Will do."

She turned, and Raven called out after her.

"Dixie?"

"Yeah?"

"Where are you going?"

"To visit a witch."

Saw someone she wasn't supposed to.

Dixie replayed her conversation with Edward Rossi over and over in her head as she carefully navigated the slick roads.

He'd told her that Lizzie was upset because she'd seen something, or *someone*, that she wasn't supposed to, and the next morning, Lizzie had awakened to a dead, black cat on her doorstep. And then Lizzie went missing.

Something was going on there, no question about it, and Dixie needed to find out what that was.

Dixie chewed on her bottom lip. Considering the new information regarding the hair tie, there was a connection between Black Magic Balik and Lizzie now, but what would be the connection between Tanya White and the witch?

She braked around a tight corner and slid on a patch of black ice. Her heart leapt through her chest.

"Dammit."

Dixie took a moment to compose herself, and then slowly accelerated, taking the next few miles extra slow. Finally, she pulled up to the cottages. She flicked off her headlights and parked next to the woods.

All four houses were dark—not a light on in Balik's.

She grabbed her bag, got out of the truck, and yanked up her hood.

What now? Knock on Balik's door and ask if she murdered Lizzie, and Tanya?

She took a deep breath, the ice-cold air burning her lungs. She quietly walked along the tree line, her boots sinking into the snow, and after taking a quick look around, she crept down the side of Balik's cottage, paused and listened.

Silence.

No witch, no black cats, no hair ties.

Her pulse picked up as she stepped onto the porch and noticed the back door was open, just a crack. Her stomach tickled with nerves—warning bells. After looking around, Dixie pulled her gun from her hip, and tiptoed to the door.

Her heart pounded as she pushed it open and listened— silence. She took a glance over her shoulder, and after a minute, stepped over the threshold and into the darkness.

The moment her boot hit the kitchen floor, a flash of movement burst from the side.

Tingles shot up her spine as she spun on her heel and raised her gun.

A body lurched toward her, the clanging of chains vibrating through the air.

Dixie jumped backward.

"Get me out of here!" A weak, raspy voice called out.

With her finger firmly on the trigger, she swallowed the knot in her throat, and said, "Who are you?"

"I'm Agnes Balik. Marden's sister."

16

*D*IXIE'S EYES ROUNDED in shock—she was staring at a woman who had been missing for forty years. As she opened her mouth to ask one of the hundred questions zooming through her head, she heard movement behind her.

She whipped around and pointed her gun at Marden Balik.

Balik, dressed head-to-toe in black, stopped, and narrowed her beady eyes.

Dixie tightened the grip on her gun. "Last time I checked, it wasn't very hospitable to chain a houseguest to the wall, Ms. Balik."

"She's no houseguest." Her voice seethed with anger. "She's a homewrecker who stole my husband from me." Like a flash of lightning, Balik grabbed a knife from the counter and swung it at Dixie.

Dixie dodged the blow, lunged forward, knocked the knife from Balik's hand and pointed the gun at her head.

"On your knees."

As she slowly kneeled, Balik's eyes darkened and locked on Dixie's.

"On your stomach."

Balik began muttering a slow, rhythmic chant as she slid onto her front.

Agnes covered her ears. "Might want to hurry, dear."

"What the hell is she singing?"

"She's *cursing* you."

Goosebumps prickled Dixie's skin.

"Might want to be extra careful tonight, dear."

Sirens screamed through the air as two police cars pulled up to the cottages.

Dixie met Zander at the front door.

"Where is she?"

"I've got Balik hog-tied on the kitchen floor, and Agnes is sitting calmly at the kitchen table—she's chained to the wall, courtesy of Balik."

Zander called out over his shoulder to a nearby officer. "They're in the kitchen!" He turned back to Dixie and shook his head in disbelief. "Marden Balik has had her sister locked up in that house for forty damn years."

"For having an affair with her husband."

"Evil witch." He paused. "An evil witch who lives next door to a girl who was just beaten to death..."

Dixie shook her head. "Marden Balik isn't our killer."

"Why do you say that?"

"Agnes swears Marden never left the house Monday night, or today. Which means she couldn't have killed Lizzie, or Tanya."

"What about the hair tie you found?"

"How the hell do you know about that?"

Zander grinned. "Max sure does love his Caramel Macchiatos."

Dixie rolled her eyes, then said, "I asked Agnes about that, too, and she said that Lizzie accidentally saw her chained to the wall the other day, as she glanced in the window while passing by the house. Marden obviously freaked out, and stole the hair tie from Lizzie's car to voodoo her, or curse her, or something. The poor black cat was part of the curse, according to Agnes."

"Sounds like the voodoo worked considering Lizzie died the next day... she's sure Balik didn't leave the house? Monday or today?"

Dixie shrugged. "I really don't think Agnes would lie to cover for her sister, who's held her captive for forty years."

Her cell phone rang and as she pulled it from her pocket, Zander put his hand on his shoulder. "Nice job solving a forty-year-old cold case, Dix."

"We've still got a serial killer to find." She stepped aside. "Dixie here."

"Yo, Dix, it's Ace. I just pulled the orders from Banshee's Brew and, bingo, we've got a special-order from a few weeks ago for a case of Chateaux LaRouse. No name, but we've got an address."

Excitement shot through her. "Give it to me."

"Six-sixty Goldview Road."

"Thanks."

Click.

Dixie jumped in her truck and pulled onto the road as an ambulance pulled in behind the police cars. Zander was in for a hell of a night.

She grabbed her cell phone and dialed Liam's number. Voicemail.

"Liam, hey it's Dixie. I've got a lead that I'm going to quickly follow-up on. If I'm not at the office when you get there, wait on me. I shouldn't be long."

She clicked off her phone and glanced at the clock—nine-thirty. According to her GPS, Goldview Road was only ten minutes away.

Adrenaline pumped through her as she drove down the road. This was her first solid lead, and something in her gut told her she was onto something.

She flicked on her turn signal and turned onto a narrow road that cut down the middle of manicured woods, snow-covered pastures and fancy wooden fences.

Dixie slowed as she neared a mailbox—660. This was it. She peered at the large, brick mansion. No lights on, no cars out front. It appeared that no one was home. She tapped the steering wheel, contemplating her next move.

Maybe just a few minutes looking around...

She flicked off the headlights, slowly drove up the drive-way, parked, and got out.

Every room was dark except for a dim glow from a back window. She glanced over her shoulder before quietly walking down the edge of the house.

Her heart began to race as she neared the window, and ignoring the nagging in her head to turn around and go back, she pressed up on her tiptoes and peered into, what appeared to be, the master bathroom.

The windowsill was lined with candles, face creams and lotions. She squinted and leaned closer—and her heart stopped.

Dixie's eyes rounded, her mouth dropped open.

Sitting in the middle of the ledge was a gold bottle named *24K Illuminator*—a luxury body lotion infused with microscopic specks of real gold.

She gasped, pushed back, and as she started to turn
—*click.*

Dixie froze as the tip of a gun pressed into the back of
her skull.

17

ITH A BAG of chicken fingers, french fries and two chocolate milkshakes, Liam turned onto the long driveway that led to Black Rose Investigations.

His phone beeped, alerting him to a new voicemail. He frowned—he must've missed a call while he was getting the food.

He listened to Dixie's message.

Shit. He shook his head. Dixie was following up on a new lead. *Dammit.* There goes his plan for keeping her in his sights until the FBI got to town.

He started to dial her number when an incoming call blinked on the screen.

"Liam here."

"Hey, it's Rick."

Something in Rick's voice had Liam's back straightening. "What's going on?"

"I got your message, but first, I just ran the list of employees at Den Care Clinic, and everyone's clean—no records, nothing suspicious. But then, I cross-referenced the list with everything I have on Terra and Maria's case and... something popped up."

His pulse picked up. "Yeah?"

"One of the employees has a vacation home in Louisiana, and according to his credit cards, he was there at the time of both Terra and Maria's murders... and he's in Devil's Den now."

His heart skipped a beat. "Give me a name."

"Edward Rossi."

Liam slammed the brakes and shoved the truck into reverse. "Get me an address."

Pause. "Liam, I called you first, but I'm going to be honest with you—the second we hang up, I'm sending this up the chain. Agents will be there within the hour."

Within the hour. Liam knew all too well how many horrific things could happen within an hour.

The truck skidded onto the road and he slammed down the gas. "What's the address, Rick?"

"Six-sixty Goldview."

"I'm on my way."

"I assumed that."

Liam hung up, ice-cold panic bursting through his veins. Is this the lead Dixie was following up on?

He sped down the road and punched the address into his GPS—he was less than seven minutes away.

He dialed Dixie's number.

"Hi, you've reached Dixie, I'm sorry I'm..."

"Dammit!" He tossed the phone on the passenger seat, gripped the steering wheel and tried to ease his racing pulse. He had to calm down. The last thing Dixie needed was his hot-headed ass hitting a patch of ice and sliding off a cliff before it was too late.

Too late.

His gut clenched.

***

Dixie's heart pounded as the gun pressed harder into her skull.

She began to slowly slide her hand into her jacket when she remembered she'd left her gun in the truck—*fuck!*

"What the hell are you doing at my house... Dixie, right? The ball-busting private investigator."

She recognized the voice—low and deep. She desperately searched her memory, but between the gun to her head, and the fear pulsing through her veins, she couldn't connect the voice to a name. She had heard it recently though, she was sure of it. And, she also had no doubt that both Lizzie Meyers and Tanya White had heard the same voice recently as well.

She clenched her jaw as anger begin to mix with the fear. She should have known—the gold specks found on the bludgeoned victims was from the murderer's luxury body cream.

Son of a bitch.

He tapped the barrel of the gun against her head. "Walk."

Her legs felt like lead weight as she took the first step.

"To the patio, to the back door."

She felt his eyes burning through her as she slowly walked down the side of the house.

He released a low groan that made her stomach curdle. "You've got less curves than I'm used to."

Her breath stopped, her eyes rounded in terror.

He continued, "Less than Lizzie and Tanya, but that's alright, as long as you can get on your knees, and open your mouth."

Dixie froze, the panic momentarily paralyzing her.

Suddenly, a blow to the back of her head had her stumbling forward.

"Let's go. Pick up the pace."

Pain pulsed through her skull, sending a fresh wave of fear through her body. Images of Lizzie and Tanya's naked bodies and bloodied heads flashed through her brain. Chill bumps ran over her arms.

No, you will not be next. You will not be his next victim.

As she stepped onto the patio, she looked for any kind of weapon. Her hands were unbound, which was to her advantage, but the gun pointed at her head, on the other hand, was not.

The spacious patio had a pool, fire pit, outdoor kitchen and covered seating area with a big screen television.

This guy had some money.

Dixie's eyes darted around the outdoor kitchen—no knives, no pots or pans, glass bottles, nothing.

Keeping looking, Dixie. There's got to be something.

"To the back door."

Do not go inside. Do not go inside. She knew that with most abduction cases, a victim's survival rate decreased significantly as soon as they got into the abductor's vehicle. She assumed a house was no different.

Panic started to take hold as she walked closer to the back door. Her mind raced trying to place the voice of the man who was forcing her into his home.

A gust of wind sent snow swirling around the potted evergreen trees that lined the wall, and her eyes landed on a small pair of pruning shears leaning against one of the pots.

Hope sparked through her. This was her chance.

As she neared the pot, her adrenaline—fear, hope, nerves—surged.

You can do this Dixie, it's your only shot.

She thought of Lizzie and Tanya and how their lives were cut mercilessly short. She would *not* be next.

Dixie lunged forward and grabbed the shears. And as she spun around to fight, the blast knocked her off her feet, sending the shears flying into the air. She landed on her back with a *thud* and everything around her became a blur. The world started to spin, the pain started to register.

The warmth of the blood began to spread over her stomach as she slipped away, into darkness.

***

Liam slid around a tight corner, and pressed the gas. He squinted to see ahead as the fences and manicured grounds zoomed past the windows.

He glanced down at the GPS—the destination was fifty-feet ahead, on the right.

His heart hammered in his chest.

Would he be too late?

Liam passed the mailbox, slammed the brakes, and turned onto the driveway.

Sweat beaded on his forehead as he skidded to a stop behind Dixie's truck. He grabbed his gun from the passenger seat and jumped out.

The hair on the back of his neck prickled—Dixie was in danger, he knew it.

Like the flick of a light, he switched to military mode. This was a recon mission... for the woman who had stolen his heart.

After one quick inhale to steady himself, he took off toward the house, moving silently along the shadows like an animal hunting its prey.

A light turned on.

He pressed his back against the wall and held his breath.

The light turned off, and then another light flicked on, in another room.

Liam moved along the side of the house, following the path of the light.

As he neared the back, he heard a door open and slap shut, and the patio light turned on.

He slid his finger over the trigger, and stealthily stepped to the very edge of the house, watching the shadow of a silhouette stretch across the yard.

It was carrying something.

He inhaled, raised his gun, and stepped out of the shadows, and faced the patio.

Shock momentarily paralyzed him.

In a pool of blood, Dixie lay motionless by the back door, and standing next to her was Edward Rossi, with a tarp slung over his shoulder.

Rage flooded his veins as he surged onto the porch.

Edward spun around—dropping the tarp—and pulled the gun from his coat.

Liam lunged forward and grabbed his arm. The gun tumbled to the ground as Edward sent an elbow into Liam's face, and kicked his gun from his hand.

Blood trickled down Liam's chin, the metallic taste seeping into his mouth. Blind with rage now, he slammed his fist into Edward's jaw, sending him stumbling backward. He grabbed Edward's shirt and punched him again, and again, and again. Blood splattered on the side of the house, and the *crunch* of Edward's nose breaking vibrated through the air. As Edward doubled-over, writhing in pain, Liam crushed his knee into Edward's face, knocking him out, and sending him tumbling off the deck.

He spun around and dropped to his knees.

"Dixie!"

His eyes darted over her body. Snowflakes dusted her long dark hair, her face was as white as a ghost.

The blood from a gunshot wound saturated her stomach.

Terror ripped through him and he grabbed his cell phone.

"I need a medic to six-sixty Goldview, now!"

18

*T*hirty-six hours later...

DIXIE OPENED HER eyes, blinking away the blurriness.

"Good morning."

His voice was as comforting as a warm embrace. She turned her head, and smiled. "Good morning."

Liam stood from his chair, which was pressed against her hospital bed. "How are you feeling?"

Dixie paused for a moment as the events of the last two days unjumbled through her medicated haze.

"I feel good, better."

He smiled. "Intravenous pain meds will do that to you. Do you want some coffee?"

"*Yes.*"

She started to push herself up and Liam gently grabbed her arm. "Wait... here, let me help." He stacked a few extra pillows behind her, lifted the bed, and eased her forward.

She winced at the pain in her stomach, although quickly remembering just how lucky she was.

Minutes after Liam had rescued Dixie from bleeding to death on Edward Rossi's patio, the house was swarmed by police, FBI agents, and medics. Dixie was rushed to the hospital where she was treated for a gunshot wound to her stomach—which, luckily had gone straight through her body, missing her internal organs. According to her doctor, the bullet missed her spleen by *"a hair."*

Luck had been on her side... well, luck and Liam Cash.

The hospital door opened and a nurse scurried in, taking a quick glance at the hunky man towering over Dixie's bed. Dixie grinned.

After recording her stats, the nurse checked Dixie's wound.

Liam slid his hand over hers as the nurse carefully lifted her gown and peeled back the bandage. As the adhesive tore away from Dixie's skin, she lightly inhaled and looked at Liam, and was startled by his expression. His jaw was set, his stance was rigid, and fire spilled from his eyes as he looked at the jagged scar on her stomach.

Dixie squeezed his hand, shaking him from the rage boiling inside of him.

Liam looked at her, his face softening minimally.

She smiled, winked.

He exhaled and seemed to relax, slightly.

The nurse placed a fresh bandage over her skin. "You're doing great, Dixie, your stitches, everything. You're healing extraordinarily quickly." Her smile faded and a look of concern washed over her face. She glanced at Liam before looking back down at Dixie. "There's some agents outside, to see you."

She inhaled, nodded. "I'm ready to talk to them."

Liam stepped forward. "Ma'am, give Dixie and me a

minute to speak before you send them in, and would you mind ordering some coffee for her, please."

"Of course." The nurse sent one more look of pity toward Dixie and then quietly left the room.

Dixie turned to Liam, knowing he was going to protest. "I want to talk to them, I promise, I'm feeling better. I can handle it. But... can you update me on everything that's happened since I've been out? I'd rather hear it from you."

He hesitated, his eyes turning ice-cold, and she could see the pain and anger the last thirty-six hours had brought him.

"Please, tell me Liam, and don't leave anything out."

After a moment, he said, "Edward is behind bars and is being charged with the murders of Terra Voss, Maria Nolen, Lizzie Meyers and Tanya White... and for attempted murder..." He paused, his cheeks flushing with anger.

"For me."

"Right." He began pacing—a feeble attempt to release the adrenaline pumping through his body.

"Is Edward talking? Confessing?"

"No. But the lotion with the gold specks in his bathroom links him to all four women, and, they found a burner phone in his house, and have confirmed that it's the phone he used to communicate with Lizzie and Tanya. They also found encrypted emails buried in his laptop. He's a psychotic son of a bitch that would play games with the girls, each love affair was a secret. A twisted, sick game. He would buy them gifts, seduce them and then kill them. And all four women looked the same—blonde hair, same personality types. They're stacking mounds of evidence against him now."

"Does he have a black truck? Marden Balik mentioned something about a black truck driving by Lizzie's recently..."

He nodded. "Yep, she confirmed his truck with a picture the FBI showed her—right before she mysteriously escaped her jail cell."

"What?"

"Yeah..." He scratched his head. "That's kind of an interesting story, actually... thirty minutes after she was interviewed, an officer found the guard passed out on the floor, with the letter *K* cut into his forehead. And her jail cell was empty—with the door closed and locked."

"Did you say *K*?"

He nodded.

"Krestel."

"Yep, that's the rumor."

"Wait, so you're saying that Marden Balik was—*is*—Krestel? The rumored witch of the Great Shadow Mountains?"

"That's what the whole town is saying. Regardless, whoever the hell she is, the police are combing the area."

"Witch or no witch, she'll hide in the mountains."

"They'll find her."

"Good luck to them." She shook her head, and then continued, "What about John Blevins? Suzie swears he was having an affair with Lizzie. She said she saw Lizzie's car at his clinic late at night, multiple times."

"Lizzie was there to see Edward, not John. John is as clean as a whistle. We checked the security cameras and it was Edward's truck that was parked in the back, and hers was in the front. I guess Suzie just assumed her husband was there. Edward would also meet Tanya late at night there too, occasionally."

Dixie shook her head. "So that's why Tanya was so jumpy when I interviewed her... she probably thought I knew about her and Edward's secret affair. And, that's why she didn't like Lizzie... she probably suspected something was going on with them, too."

The room fell silent as Dixie tried to digest the disturbing information.

Liam walked to her bedside, grabbed, and squeezed her hand. "Look, Dixie, you don't have to talk if you're not ready. Trust me, they'll wait as long as you need."

She shook her head. "No, I want to now. Right now. I want this done and behind me. My interview will help things move faster. I feel better, I can do this."

"I thought you'd say that." He exhaled, leaned down and lightly stroked her hair. "You're so strong, Dixie. You, your body... you're so strong."

She looked up, surprised at the emotion in his voice.

He continued, "I'm so sorry I didn't get there earlier—

"Liam, you saved my life. You literally saved my life. I wouldn't be here without you."

He opened his mouth to speak, but she cut him off and said, "No more discussion about that, okay? I'll be forever grateful for you..." Tears welled in her eyes. "You saved my life."

A single tear glistened in Liam's eye right before he leaned down, and kissed her softly on the lips. He pulled away, his face inches from hers, his eyes full of emotion.

He whispered, "I love you, Dixie. I know it's crazy, but I love you."

Her heart swelled, her breath stopped. Shock spread over her face.

"You do?"

He smiled, sniffed. "Yes, dammit, I do."

She smiled, tears swimming in her eyes.

"I love you too, Liam."

****

Grab your copy of the the next book in the series, HATCHET HOLLOW, today!

★ HER MERCENARY ★

WHAT'S NEXT?

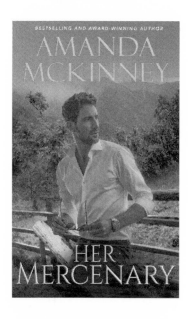

The bestselling and award-winning Steele Shadows series

continues in this new **Protector Romance** *spin-off series, packed with page-turning mystery, steamy angst, exotic locations, and four, dangerously attractive mercenaries.*

She was supposed to be the mission. She became his undoing.

When American schoolteacher Samantha Greene goes missing in Mexico, the US government calls on private military firm, Astor Stone Inc., to assist in finding her. Former soldier Roman Thieves volunteers for the case, seizing the opportunity to kill two birds with one stone. After-all, no one knows the dark underworld of human trafficking like he does—or knows exactly how involved he is in their business dealings.

When the mission falls apart, Roman finds himself on the run with the blonde-haired, green-eyed bombshell, seeking refuge in the untamed wilderness of the Sierra Madre Mountains—on a trail rumored to be haunted, nonetheless. With only a small bag of provisions, they must battle the elements, including scorching hot temperatures, and work together to outsmart the savage predators hunting them.

As his motives become clouded by a fierce need to protect Sam, Roman must choose between avenging his past and saving the woman who snuck her way into his heart.

Each book is a standalone Romantic Suspense, no cliffhangers.

PREORDER NOW

Sign up for my newsletter to be the first to receive details on this emotional and twisted new small-town mystery romance...

♥ *And don't forget to sign up for my blogging team!* ♥

ABOUT THE AUTHOR

Amanda McKinney is the bestselling and multi-award-winning author of more than twenty romantic suspense and mystery novels. Her book, Rattlesnake Road, was named one of *POPSUGAR's 12 Best Romance Books to Have a Spring Fling With,* and was featured on the *Today Show.* The fifth book in her Steele Shadows series was recently nominated for the prestigious *Daphne du Maurier Award for Excellence in Mystery/Suspense.* Amanda's books have received over fifteen literary awards and nominations.

Set in small, Southern towns, Amanda writes page-turning murder mysteries peppered with steamy romance. She lives in Arkansas with her handsome husband, two beautiful boys, and three obnoxious dogs.

Text **AMANDABOOKS to 66866** to sign up for Amanda's Newsletter and get the latest on new releases, promos, and freebies!

www.amandamckinneyauthor.com

If you enjoyed Devil's Gold, please write a review!

THE AWARD-WINNING BERRY SPRINGS SERIES
The Woods (A Berry Springs Novel)
The Lake (A Berry Springs Novel)
The Storm (A Berry Springs Novel)
The Fog (A Berry Springs Novel)
The Creek (A Berry Springs Novel)
The Shadow (A Berry Springs Novel)
The Cave (A Berry Springs Novel)

#1 BESTSELLING STEELE SHADOWS
Cabin 1 (Steele Shadows Security)
Cabin 2 (Steele Shadows Security)
Cabin 3 (Steele Shadows Security)

Phoenix (Steele Shadows Rising)
Jagger (Steele Shadows Investigations)
Ryder (Steele Shadows Investigations)
★ *Her Mercenary (Steele Shadows Mercenaries), coming May 2022* ★

Rattlesnake Road
Redemption Road

The Viper

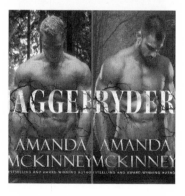

Like your sexy murder mysteries with a side of evil witch? Check out THE BLACK ROSE MYSTERY SERIES about three super-rich, independent, badass sisters who run a private investigation company in a creepy, southern town...

Devil's Gold (A Black Rose Mystery, Book 1)

READING ORDER GUIDE

SMALL-TOWN MYSTERY ROMANCE

Steele Shadows Security Series:
*Action-packed Romantic Suspense with swoon-worthy military heroes and smart, sassy heroines. Must be read in order.
First-person POV.*
#1 Cabin 1
#2 Cabin 2
#3 Cabin 3
#4 Phoenix (Steele Shadows Rising) - Can be read as a standalone.

Steele Shadows Investigations Series:
Action-packed Romantic Suspense/Crime Thriller. Each book is a standalone. First-person POV.
#1 Jagger
#2 Ryder

Steele Shadows Mercenaries Series:

*Action-packed Protector Romance. Mystery, Exotic Locations,
Swoony Heroes. Each book is a standalone. First-person POV.*
#1 *Her Mercenary*
#2 *Her Renegade*

Road Series:
*Dark, emotional Romantic Suspense/Mystery. Each book is a
standalone. First-person POV.*
#1 *Rattlesnake Road*
#2 *Redemption Road*

Berry Springs Series:
*Romantic Suspense/Mystery. Each book is a standalone.
Third-person POV.*
The Woods
The Lake
The Storm
The Fog
The Creek
The Shadow
The Cave

Broken Ridge Series:
*Action-packed Romantic Suspense with swoon-worthy heroes
and smart, sassy heroines. Must be read in order.
First-person POV.*
#1 *The Viper*
#2 *The Recluse*

Black Rose Mysteries:
*Romantic Suspense novellas. Must be read in order.
Third-person POV.*

#1 Devil's Gold
#2 Hatchet Hollow
#3 Tomb's Tale
#4 Evil Eye
#5 Sinister Secrets

Made in the USA
Columbia, SC
19 August 2022